DON'T GO IN ALONE!

"Jesus of all creation! What the *hell* was that?"

They stared through the glass in the door at the maelstrom that consumed the other chamber.

Ed trembled. "It's what I said. It's our fate, our karma. You can't change it. Nobody can." He shook his head. "We'll never get out of here alive."

"It's some kind of fish. But where the hell did they come from?" said Cliff. "And how come we didn't see them before? Man, that was close."

Carm shook her head, turned and fell back against the door. "*Serrasalsus Hollandi.*"

"Piranhas! But how–"

A thump sounded on the other side of the door. Carm jumped and Melanie peered through the aperture–she shrieked and jerked back. George's face slammed onto the glass, more skull than flesh. Bloody hands scraped the glass, the eyes glaring drunkenly at them. 'My world,' the jaws mouthed...

"A terrifically fun read! In *Frenzy*, Glenn Lazar Roberts takes the ideas of the physicist Stephen Wolfram on cellular automata and pushes them to the limit, weaving a tightly plotted thriller that is perfect for hard-core science fiction buffs."
    —*SiriusReviews.com*

"A plot worthy of the movies! *Frenzy* by Glenn Lazar Roberts is a perfect example of building tension… Just when you think you have it all figured out, the plot twists again and sends you giddily in a different direction."
    —Michael Fox, author of *Theater Boy*

"Glenn Lazar Roberts' fabulist thriller [has] skillfully woven topical issues—cancer research, technology, fraud—through a hair-raising plot. Frenzy is a super story. The reader turns pages eagerly right up to the astounding resolution. A must-read."
    —Carolyn Thorman, author of *Holy Orders*.

"Hip entertainment for sci-fi buffs. Glenn Lazar Roberts' *Frenzy* is a fast-paced sci-fi thriller. Using a witty and satiric style, Roberts introduces us to…science gone too far. An entertaining work of speculative fiction that provides a great deal of food for thought."
    —John Dizon, author of *Tiara*.

by

Glenn Lazar Roberts

Dark Lotus Books

Home of the
JUST PLAIN WEIRD

www.amazon.com/Glenn-Lazar-Roberts/e/B00KXX4MBW

www.darklotusbooks.com

© 2001 by Glenn L. Roberts.
First printing 2016, Dark Lotus Books.
All rights reserved.
ISBN 978-967580920
www.darklotusbooks.com

Also by
Glenn Lazar Roberts
Heroic Fantasy in the tradition of
Robert E. Howard &
Edgar Rice Burroughs

THE MAALSTROM SERIES:

BOOK 1
MAALSTROM

On the planet Maalstrom, Flores of the Turlicum battles rivals in the City of Ven and discovers a secret entrance to the forbidden Temple where he falls in love with Amina, the most beautiful gila of the Three Valleys.

BOOK 2
THE SELK KING

Amina is abducted by the silent winged malkops and flown to their city in the clouds. Flores crosses half a world to find her, building to a shattering climax, in another plot of unexpected twists and turns.

More of the
JUST PLAIN WEIRD
from **DARK LOTUS BOOKS:**

A tale of the fantastic
and macabre...

THE GLOW

by

Glenn Lazar Roberts

Sam Trencher has a problem. To keep from exploding into flames, he must keep the exact same coins in each pocket. Six years ago he left his home town and his girl. Now he's coming back to find her—but can't tell what's real and what's not...and his temperature is rising.

AND COMING SOON!
*More fevered dreams
from the mind of*
Glenn Lazar Roberts...

Chapter 1

The video glowed. Drawing her covers down, Carm rolled to view the computer screen beside her bed. With the sound turned off, it worked as well as an alarm clock, the light alone serving to rescue her from her dreams. She opened one eye to view the Weather Channel.

The Big One was closer.

She stretched one arm to see the voicemail in print. Clicked. Several messages materialized. 'Carmy, we need all employees to report to work as usual, and for extended hours, even though we'll be shutting down the Project early...'

Damn.

'Hello, parent. This is your school district. We're closing all schools for the next three days...'

Damn again.

'Hey, baby, I'm back in town, but stuck on the other side of the Interstate. The traffic's murder. You're on your own with your kids. See you at your office tonight.'

Damn three and I'm out. She rolled back and drew the covers over her eyes.

The covers slid down of their own accord.

"Hi Cheyenne."

The pretty ten-year-old tow-headed girl hugged Carm and kissed her on the cheek. "Early bird, Mom. You know how my teacher hates for me to be late."

"No school today, dear. But I have to go to work."

Her mouth dropped open. "That's not fair." She stamped a foot.

"Tell your brother–"

"Mom..." Burke, a brown-haired, sleepy-eyed boy of eight schlepped into the room. "I want... I want..." He rubbed his eyes. "... you." He slid into bed with her.

"We have to hurry, kids," she said between kisses. "I'm taking you to Miss Mary's today."

They had convulsions. "Not that place! Miss Mary is mean. And the kids are all ignorant."

"No choice, gang. Now throw on some clothes. You know the routine." Carm slipped on a robe. "And Carl won't be here."

"Who?" said Burke.

"That's not funny. Your new father, that's who."

"So he won't be here. Like that's a surprise," added Cheyenne. "We've seen him how many times since you married him–three?"

Carm paused, glanced at them, but said nothing. No need to state the obvious.

FRENZY

In a few minutes they dressed, wolfed down breakfast, and headed for the car. The sky was clear. The kind of clear that locals knew and feared, with small wisps of cirrus moving quickly as if propelled by some remote disturbance. Carm recalled the weather report. The Big One had finally come. No more smug complacency; no more wishful thinking. This was the real thing, the kind of hurricane that could crush a city in hours and rip corpses from graveyards to mingle with the newly drowned. It was due tonight, and the freeways were jammed with snowbirds, for once fleeing with good reason. Only a few 'lucky' employees remained behind at the command of their sovereigns.

Carm inserted the key. For a moment, she wished the engine would stall. She could then unload the kids and go back inside. But the Project called. Besides, the Institute and the daycare were much safer than her home today, both inside buildings. She glanced about the street. Most of the neighbors had evacuated. Only a few stragglers were still loading up.

Cheyenne climbed into the front seat. A book dropped and she looked at Carm.

"Not Russian again. You said you would stick with French."

"But I like the funny letters."

"Your teacher hates it when you talk Russian. She knows French."

"All right, Mom." She opened her French book. Inside

was hidden Russian, belying the picture of Victor Hugo on the cover.

"That's better."

A shadow passed overhead to a loud buzz.

"We don't have time, Burke."

From the back seat, Burke aimed a radio transmitter. A moment later a toy copter nose-dived through the open car window and was snared by a net.

"One day you'll miss. And you'll owe me a paint job."

"Yeah, when I'm old and tired, like–"

"Say it and die."

Burke exchanged a silent smile with Cheyenne while Carm backed out.

She stole a few minutes of calm listening to the tires hum, thankful that the children were quiet. For once. Twenty minutes later a gust of moist wind whipped up as they stepped out of the car at Miss Mary's. Through her office window, Carm could see Mary scowl. All right, so her kids were different. That did not make them bad. And yes, she did not come regularly because she did not approve of daycares unless they were absolutely necessary. But she paid the bill as if they did. And yes, she was often late, to drop them off and to pick them up. After all, she's a single Mom. Or was she? She sighed. She no longer knew the answer to that.

She got out to walk the children in. The thought recurred: *Why can't Mary meet us at the car? She's just standing there, watching. A little customer relations wouldn't kill her and it would save me a lot of time and energy*. Carm hurried the children forward, colliding with several others entering with kids, or coming back out. A quick apology, and she took Cheyenne and Burke inside.

"I've got to work late tonight, Mary. You're holding special hours like you said, aren't you?"

Mary nodded. She lifted a finger. "But only to eight o'clock. I'm telling you like I'm telling everyone else. You must pick them up by eight, because I may be leaving town. I haven't decided yet whether we're evacuating. Depends on the storm. And late means a dollar a minute."

"I'll be here, don't worry. No later than eight."

Within moments she was inside her car pulling into the street. Her car turned a corner and vanished.

"Did you touch them?" Fingering something in his pocket, a short man with eyes round like an owl ceased staring at the spot where Carm's car had last been visible, and turned to look at his companion. A taller, older woman whose hair was stealthily turning gray continued to stare up and beyond the horizon. Slowly she nodded. They turned and walked toward an old car parked across the road.

The first sheets of rain fell as Carm's cell phone rang.

"'Lo."

"Carm, gal. This is your gorgeous new husband."

"Hi, Carl. Did you finish your deliveries?"

"And how! Listen, beautiful. The traffic here is starting to break up, so I'm heading to Sweats-R-Us. They've got an extra room where I can get some shut-eye. Then I've got to visit a friend. I called to ask if you remember that party you said you wanted."

The rain blinding her, she juggled wipers, phone, and steering wheel. A red light saved her from disaster. She stopped the car and focused. "I never said I wanted a party, Carl. I'm busy at work. But if you want to have one, I guess we can plan it."

"No need baby. It's on for tonight. I talked to some friends and they'll be on the top floor of the Institute by eight o'clock. We're having a hurricane party! An all-nighter!"

"At my office? Wait a minute–"

"Ciao, gorgeous. Don't thank me now, thank me later. I'll see ya before it starts."

"Carl, I'm not sure that's a good idea. Carl? Carl…"
Silence.

She started forward again. "I thought strikes only came in threes," she mumbled, shutting off the phone.

The road led through a tunnel. For a moment the downpour halted, but the underpass lights were out and she was unable to see anything but the red brake lights of the car in front as traffic slowed to a crawl. Something within her chilled and she was relieved when she exited. The violence of the incoming storm was preferable to the darkness of her dreams.

Another ten minutes and she pulled into the parking garage of the Institute. Another twenty, and she was calculating aquaculture nutrients on a computer in her office on the twelfth floor. Although her body remained seated before the computer screen, clothed in her usual white lab coat, her mind traveled far away, oblivious of the sterile hospital clock that circled round and round like a force of nature.

Seven o'clock chimed and a familiar knock sounded on her door bringing her back to reality. With a shock she noticed the time. Carl sauntered in.

"Baby, look at you!" He landed a wet kiss on her lips. "I don't have to tell you what a catch you are." He spread her arms. "Oh, baby! What a shame I can't spend every minute in town. But if I did, neither of us would ever leave home."

"Nice to see you too." She kissed him back. "About the party, Carl–"

"Not to worry. I'll be back in time. Just have to run across town to take care of some more business."

"Again?"

"The bills won't pay themselves, dear. Got to make the moolah somehow."

"But you said you were off today."

"But still tending to business, as always."

She turned, flicked the computer to the Weather Channel. "You do know that this is no ordinary hurricane."

Leaning over her, he looked at the screen. He whistled. "So how long do I have?"

"One hour–tops." She gathered her black hair into a tail and flipped it smartly through a band. Rising, she abandoned the dense swirls of white on the computer screen to view the real thing through the window. The rain now came in torrents.

"Hell, that's plenty of time. I'll be back in half an hour." Carl beamed the pretty boy smile that had so entranced her in a former life. He tugged at one sleeve of his leather jacket, inspected his teeth in its shiny newness, and made for the door.

"Better hurry. The rain is just beginning. It will get worse once the first spiral comes over."

"Well what's your problem? You wanted a party didn't you? You can't have a hurricane party without a hurricane. Besides, a little water never hurt anyone." He jerked the door-knob.

"*You* wanted the hurricane party, Carl. And those will be *your* friends out there whooping it up–except for the wage slaves like me who are stuck here for the night."

He grinned again. "Life's a bitch, ain't it?" Carl sucked in the moisture that penetrated the top floor of the medical research building, despite the sealed windows. He let it out in satisfaction. "And this bitch is *mine*!" He blew her a kiss and strutted down the hall.

"And remember what you promised last week–you're supposed to pick up Cheyenne and Burke! By eight o'clock. Sharp!"

"Don't worry about your little darlings. I'll bring em

back alive. We can't have them making someone else's life miserable, now can we?" The lift rang and he was gone.

Carm stood a moment contemplating the wet expanse of sky. The Big One had finally hit. And Carl wanted to party! She returned to the aquaculture nutrients and shook her head. How did he always manage to get the day off when she had to work?

Chapter 2

When the roaring of the wind grew too loud to concentrate, Carm shut down her computer and turned off the surge protector. From habit. Between kids and the Project, lightning was the least of her worries. She glanced at the wall. Eight o'clock. Carl was late, and the violence of the storm increasing. Carm wondered what was so important that he needed to tend to it just before all hell broke loose, but at least he did promise to get the kids, which saved her having to beg off work.

A gust of wind beat on the window. She tapped one finger. She had better call. Picking up the phone, she put it down to find the number of the daycare, then picked it up again. Paused. She tapped the connectors. Then put the receiver down. No dial tone. She wished she could fire off an email but the daycare had none–if one could believe that. And the Institute did not allow cell phones. Primal was the word. Or had been. Now, apparently, it was patience.

Down the hall, the whooping was already up. A dozen people stood by a huge glass window gazing northward across the mile-wide park that stretched toward city center. Carm recognized some; knew none by name.

"Hi. I'm Carm."

A black man in brown slacks slightly taller than her broke into a pleasant smile. "Name's Cliff." He shook her hand. "Carm, have you ever seen the likes of this?"

"Can't say I have." She pressed her face to the glass. "The streets are flooding." She pursed her lips. "And the lightning. Hurricanes don't usually have lightning. Just wind and rain."

"Yeah, it's a strange one. And they say stronger than we've seen in a century. Well, we're stuck here now. I thought I'd just have a beer and mosey out of town once the traffic eased up."

Carm shook her head. "Too late." Her face lit with a lightning flash. "What do you do when you're not mosey-ing?"

"Program computers. And take them apart." He flashed the smile again. "And sometimes put them back together." He stared out the window. "I thought I'd visit my Aunt Martha in Dallas. She's got cancer."

Two young men in outback shorts and Izods yelled.

"Hot damn, Terry!" shouted one after a lightning flash. "Did ya see that one?"

"Whoa!" answered Terry.

"Married?" Carm continued. "Children?"

"No and no. I'd really be worried if I did. On a night like this, I mean, who would risk their life at a hurricane party if they had someone at home who needed them?"

"Yeah. Who?" Her eyes turned away to search for another clock.

Two beers popped. The outback pair looked at Cliff.

He shrugged. "Why not? Looks like I'll definitely be

here awhile." He accepted one and took a long drink.

Cliff looked at Carm and she shook her head.

"Good! That means more for us."

The pair turned back to the window.

"There's another good one! Just like when we fragged them camel jockeys in the Gulf."

A green-eyed woman with too much lipstick turned a languid stare. "Well, give me another beer, Cracker. I don't want to get stuck with the driving."

Cracker fished a can from a well-stocked cooler. "One cold beer for one hot mama."

"Too late. Mel. I'm way ahead of you." The other took a swig and tossed some keys to the woman. She caught them and dropped them in the cooler. "Did you just go deaf, Terry? I said I don't feel like driving."

Terry fished the keys out of the water and tested the buttons. "Cripes Melanie. That's wasteful. Now the electronics won't work."

"So what? You do your laundry by hand just to show how tough you are. Now you can use the key. Big deal. Everything's wet anyway."

Terry stood taller. "You know, just because men put dollars in your G-string doesn't make you God's gift." Melanie ignored him and drank her beer.

Cracker smiled. "Forget it man, it's history. But you're right–only jockeys should be wasted." Cracker and Terry guffawed and slapped palms.

A moment earlier the elevator bell had rung and they

turned to stare at a short man with round eyes, and an older woman with graying hair.

"It's history, alright," the man said. "It's the end of the world. Nostradamus said hurricanes would come. Edgar Cayce too. They both warned that the weather would change. They warned everyone."

The outback pair exchanged smirks.

"Not Nostradamus, Ed." said the woman. "Only Cayce. Nostradamus lived a long time ago."

"Yes, but he saw things. He saw the future. He knew what was coming."

"What about El Nino?" said Cliff. "Some people say that's responsible."

Ed looked at Cliff. "That's part of it. But not all. *They* knew. *They* understood. There are big changes coming."

The older woman spoke. "Pay no attention to Ed, he likes to read about psychics." Carm felt a strange thrill rise along her spine, unaccountably since her knowledge of psychics was limited to gypsies in infomercials whose only talent was reading credit cards.

"Where did you guys meet Carl?" she asked.

Ed and his companion looked at each other.

"Well, do you work around here?"

"Marlena invited me."

The woman looked back at Ed. "No, Ed. *You* invited *me.*"

Ed looked gloomy. "See what I mean. It's fate. You'll meet your end wherever your karma decides. You can't change it. No one can. Not you. Not me. Not Marlena. And she even knows how she is going to die."

"Oh, Ed." She looked back and laughed. "I have visions," she confided to the others. "We were parking the car earlier when I heard voices telling us to find a safer place." She smiled contentedly, as if all was now explained.

"There is no safe place. Cayce said all the coastlines would be under water, and half the country. It's not water that will kill her, but something else." He glanced at her. "She knows but she won't tell."

The trees in the park rippled before a gust. The lift rang again and Carm rushed into the corridor.

"Cheyenne! Burke!" She stopped short.

Out of the elevator stepped a weather-worn man of about thirty with an auburn beard, in pressed overalls and a Western hat. Beside him was a dark-haired too-good-looking younger and taller figure dressed in a state-of-the-wallet Armani suit. Their shoes echoed as the latter put distance between them.

"Yep, I'm telling you, the weed's what did it."

"You don't say." The suit spoke without glancing back.

"I do. One day I was baking pot brownies when it came to me. Bake the chips before shipping them out. Like boot camp. Only the strong survive. The failure rate of the chips dropped so low that the box makers all jumped on board and placed orders with me."

The suit paused, then bit. "You supply computer chips

to computer retailers?"

"No, man. 'Box makers.' They make cardboard boxes out of chips these days. Federal subsidies–back to nature and all that."

"You mean..."

"Yeah, man. Cows. You're not from around here are you?"

"You must be Bill," Carm butted in.

"Wild Bill," he grinned.

"Carl said you have more hair than sense."

"I resemble that remark." He removed his hat to expose a gleaming pate. "Lost every one at goddam nineteen years old."

"I know," she added. "Life's a bitch."

Bill beamed with unexpected pleasure. "Made my first hundred thousand in packaging and boxes, then got into commercial construction."

They winced as a crash of thunder rolled over. Carm glanced at Bill's companion.

"Gary." Gold cufflinks glinted on his outstretched wrist.

"I'm Carm." Gary gave her the once over and she awkwardly smoothed her lab coat. From habit. Her figure was sleek and neither two children nor a frumpy gown halted the inspections she had endured since puberty. Once that had meant something. Before two honeymoons. Now it was just another part of the Former Life.

"No name tags? How are we supposed to keep score?"

He smiled.

"I work for the Institute. But don't let that fool you, I'm as human as you."

"Or Bob."

"Bill."

Carm took the cue. "You were telling us what you do."

Bill grabbed both by the shoulder. "You're standing on it!"

Startled, they glanced down, looking for who knows what.

"Who do you think built this place?"

Eyebrows rose.

"I mean this floor of the Institute–this addition," added Bill.

"ABI Construction, locally headquartered, a recent incorporation," Gary recited.

"Which sub-contracted the work to..."

Gary's eyes rolled back to examine memory banks. "Wild Construction..."

"Wild *Bill* Construction." Bill smiled and stroked his beard.

Carm laughed. "That's right. You handled the rewiring last winter. I remember."

Wild Bill grinned and rocked on his heels.

"Do you work for ABI?" Carm asked Gary.

Gary whipped out a card like a magician. "Frost, Lank, and Frere. IP."

Bill looked puzzled. "I thought you were a lawyer."

"Intellectual Property," he explained. "We represent biotech firms with their industrial relations."

Bill brightened. "So you *are* the honcho I want. Tell me: what do I do about this goldang architect who keeps calling me about the rewiring job? The wiring is fine, the maintenance bozos just don't know how to work the timers."

Gary gazed down his nose. "Bob–"

"Bill."

"Bill, before I could give you an answer I would have to look at every aspect of your case, not only contracts but every communication that has passed between you and ABI." He eyed Bill's attire. "Are you on a budget?"

"We're at a party, man. You can drop me a freebie."

Gary smiled. "Look, let me share something with you, uh..."

"Bill."

"The first thing I learned in law school was 'You can't help the economics.' The fees are the fees. The second was 'It's unethical to give away what someone somewhere can pay for.' Did you know that I can be sued for free advice as well as paid?"

Bill put his hands in his pockets.

"The third was 'Stick to what you know.' Now if you like, I can refer you to a friend of mine who is looking for your kind of work. No experience. But cheap."

Gary thumbed through some business cards. Another boom crashed and the cards sprayed in the air. Shaken,

Bill and Gary stepped into the party room. A series of gusts shook the building.

"Well if that don't put the dime in the dimebox. Will you look at that?" Bill pulled his hat more firmly onto his skull, and stared open-mouthed as sheets of wood and metal flew past despite their great height.

After a minute the wind abated and they breathed easier. Cautiously Carm approached the window. She peered down to where the streets were filling, far below, looking for the gleam of a leather jacket and two smaller, sweeter figures. Carl was athletic and knew the area well. He was a courier, so he met many people. He had a knack for gaining their confidence, and had no problem collecting an instant crowd for parties. This induced a familiar pang of guilt. Setting up parties was supposed to be the wife's job. But she was more comfortable with computers than people, which was why she had protested so weakly when Carl had announced the party. She did wish to socialize, provided she was on home ground, and the party would not neglect her Project in the Cancerous Institute. Correction—the MacDonald Cancer Research Institute. No, she decided, 'Cancerous' was better. Despite the potential benefits of her research, that was how she thought of it, especially when you-know-who was around.

High-heels clicked from the direction of the lift. "Is this where the party's at?" Gum popped.

Carm stopped smiling. Think of the devil and she appears.

FRENZY

Alice let out a bright happy laugh, then her face resumed its habitual sternness, reminding Carm of the happy and sad masks in a Greek play but with stern replacing sad. Alice was always either bright and happy or hard and stern. Sometimes in rapid succession. It was weird. And neither was any warning of her real mood.

Alice sighted Carm and the happy face appeared. "Looking for you, Carmy!"

Carm suppressed a sigh. God, how she hated that nickname. "Been right here. Watching the rain."

"Way cool!" She surveyed the scene. "Lovely weather. But we'll have to check the Pharm."

"I thought we were shutting it down early."

"No chance, Carmy. Boss-man changed his mind. Storm or no storm, he wants the Pharm running around the clock. This town may be pulling in the sidewalks, but the big boys in New York and Zurich won't even pause for breath."

Carm did not have to ask who Boss-man was. Carm and Alice had been equals until Alice had managed to get half her salary paid by Primal Lab and won Boss-man's ear. Now Alice was in charge of *her* project, which was ironic since Alice was not only less educated, but more recently hired. And younger, which perhaps explained things best.

The wind blew harder and jolted Carm out of her reverie. "I'm worried, Alice. Carl should have been back by now with my kids. Maybe I should go."

"You're too late, Carmy." The gum smacked again. "The streets are knee-deep. Don't worry, I'm sure your hubby got them in time."

As if to emphasize what she said, another gust shook the building, stronger than before. Cliff glanced nervously around. "I don't think I like this. Can the building take it?"

"Sure!" Alice beamed her happy face. "What could be safer than the Institute. It's been here forever."

"Built in 1949," added Gary.

Another gust shook them.

"Well, the Pharm *is* in the basement." Alice drifted toward the door and the others followed. The stern face was on.

"What farm?" asked Cliff.

Carm answered. "With a 'ph'. Pharm for pharmaceutical. As in Old MacDonald had one."

Cliff mouthed an Oh of comprehension. Carm continued, enjoying the attention. "The Pharm. Alias the Factory–the Monster-Mash–the Castle. I've head em all."

Alice fell silent and glanced behind her. Carm's voice continued with a nervous life of its own while her mind conjured visions of her children laboring through the storm.

"And Boss-man," Carm continued, "that's Nicholas MacDonald. He built the Institute from scratch years ago. Alias Frankenstein."

"Then that must make you Igor," said a voice.

"Either me or Alice. Though that would properly be

Igora. Or Igorette." Carm turned and felt the chill return, this time accompanied by butterflies. She knew that voice.

Behind Alice appeared a poster-boy for the city morgue, a man so anciently aged that only the laying on of hands could explain the lack of a walker. And dressed to kill. He grinned in his best suit like one determined not to miss his last adventure. Boss-man.

"Glad you could make it, Gary," Nicholas MacDonald said, his voice trembling. He offered a palsied hand to the lawyer. "I was afraid the airport might turn you away."

"Not a chance, sir. Arab terrorists on wild horses couldn't do that."

"Miss Niles, could you join us please."

Carm felt suddenly shy as a child. "Sir, I should apologize–"

"Nonsense," MacDonald shut her up. "As one of my best team players I order you not to give it a second thought." A grand-paternal smile shone beneath a shock of white hair and glinting eyes. He pulled Carm and Alice closer and whispered. "Great news! Tomorrow Primal Lab is buying out the Institute. The whole shcbang. The papers will be signed at noon." He paused to cough. "This guy," he winked at Gary, "is here to check out the system and make sure everything works. I want you to take him downstairs and show him the... 'Monster-Mash'." He eyed Carm. "Meanwhile, I will be attending the Mayor's reelection campaign at the Emporia."

"Mr. MacDonald, I don't think I can–"

He peered down at her. "This is important, Miss Niles."

"My children, sir. Cheyenne and Burke. They are stuck at my daycare. My husband–"

A loud crack startled them. Carm looked up expecting to see the accompanying flash of light in the gathering darkness. It did not come.

"Look!" gasped Alice. Across the face of the window a huge fracture had appeared. The fracture grew tendrils that raced across the plate with unnerving speed. Instinctively they backed up. In the spider-web faces of death took shape, merged, leered. For a moment there was silence but for the assault of the storm on the fractured window, sniffing like some beast for a way to enter.

Someone screamed.

With a crash the window gave way. Splinters ricocheted off the back wall, spotting it with blood. Wind and rain suddenly hammered them, and the building shuddered as a succession of explosions signaled the shattering of windows on other floors. Carm felt a hand grasp her collar and she was partly dragged, partly blown by the wind down the hall to halt in the elevator amid a crush of bodies. As the doors shut, the lights went out.

Chapter 3

When the lift rang all was quiet. Carm opened her eyes and stared as fluorescent lights cycled on and off. A blue blur obscured her vision and, although she lay on her side, she jerked backwards.

"Oh...Ruben." She struggled to her feet. A young man in blue medical scrubs helped her up, then flicked light switches on the wall several times. The lights burned steady again.

"You all right?"

"I think so." She looked down. "Oh my god."

Terry lay in a pool of blood.

Cracker took an arm. "Are you okay?" The three helped Terry stand and brushed off dust and broken glass.

Cracker helped steady Melanie as she leaned against the side of the elevator. She shook him off. "Son of a bitch. Let go of me." She raised one hand to her forehead then stared in shock at the back of her hand. "I'm bleeding!"

"Not badly," observed Carm. "But your friend here is."

Terry inspected his arm and discovered several protruding glass shards. He gasped.

"They're small, buddy. You're lucky. This could be your face."

"Get em out, man!" yelled Terry. "Get em out now!"

Ed and Marlena stood and brushed themselves off, and were soon joined by Gary and Bill, soaked but unharmed.

Cracker took Terry's arm to remove the shards.

Terry pulled back. "I need professional help, man. Ask the lady doc."

"I'm not that kind of doctor," said Carm.

He looked confused. "But–you got a white coat."

"Doctor of research. Academic only."

Gary said, "Ph.D., M.I.T., Microbiology, 3.8 G.P.A." He glanced at Carm. "Never finished dissertation."

Everyone looked at Gary.

"Ouch!" Cracker removed one of the shards from Terry.

"Shut up, wus."

"It hurts, man!"

Bill attempted to shake his hat dry, but only succeeded in getting Gary wetter. "I thought you were in Iraq."

"I drove a supply truck, alright? I signed up for three square meals, not to have broken glass thrown at me."

Cracker pulled another and Terry gritted his teeth. After the last was out he whimpered.

"Well. What about me, asshole?"

Cracker looked at Melanie.

"Not you, asshole. That asshole. The one I'm married to."

"I'm hit, Mel. I'm down for the count."

She snorted. "As if you were ever up."

Terry pulled a handkerchief out of his pocket and, despite his hurt arm, dabbed Mel's forehead and hand.

She snatched it, finished it herself, and threw it back at him. "I need a mirror."

Alice emerged from behind a door a few feet away, pulling on a dry sweater. "In there. The coat room has one."

Melanie took her up while Cracker wrapped the handkerchief around Terry's arm to halt the bleeding.

"What is this place?" asked Ed nervously.

"The Institute's basement," said Ruben.

They gazed across a broad dimly lit interior dominated by a matrix of metallic totems. An electronic Stonehenge, blue and white computer servers stretched row by column to the far corners of the room. Without warning, the lights failed, and they sucked their breath, again in darkness. A constellation of red motes glowed.

Ruben muttered. "Don't worry. The emergency backup kicked in some time ago. The Array is still online." He flicked the wall switches again and the overheads came on, cycled twice, then shined steady. "It's been doing that."

Someone whistled.

"Quite a setup you got here, doc." Cracker and Gary wandered down the aisle, eyeing the apparatus.

"Ruben keeps them running," said Carm.

Melanie returned and walked back to the elevator. The doors remained open where Ruben had pulled the stationary switch. She pushed the switch back in, punched one of the floor buttons, and waited for the doors to close.

Nothing happened.

She punched again.

"Dammit!" She jammed the buttons hard.

"You don't have to break em, Mel."

"Then get me the hell outa here, asshole."

Bill stepped closer. "What for? There's nothing but a whole bunch of water up there now. You got nowhere to go, unless you came by canoe."

"He's right," added Carm. "There's nothing to do until the storm blows over. Besides, the elevators only go down when the Array is on. Not up."

"That's all right," said Terry. "We can take the stairs." Terry headed for a metal door with a jagged universal symbol emblazoned. He yanked the door handle with his good arm. It did not budge. Melanie and Cracker added their strength but all three failed to open it.

"I don't believe this, man. How do you get out of this joint?"

"You don't," said Ruben. "The security system down here is foolproof. Nobody can leave till the timer times out."

"That's just great. And whose bright idea was that?" asked Cracker.

"Anyway," added Melanie, "you can't keep us here. It's against the law. And there's fire regulations, in case you haven't heard."

"Wrong regs," said Gary. "There's no city jurisdiction

here." He finished draping his jacket over the computer exhaust outtake to dry.

"I'm afraid so," added Carm. "Due to the Array."

"How long will we be down here? When will the timers time out?" asked Ed.

Ruben answered. "The security system is designed to impose a quarantine of twenty-four hours whenever the Array is working. To prevent accidental contamination."

"That's why all of the offices–and phone lines–are upstairs," explained Carm.

"This is nuts!" Cracker approached Ruben. "Ya know what, jack? You're startin' to sound like a jockey. And that means you got a problem, buddy."

Ruben stepped behind Carm and stared.

"Contamination?" Ed looked at Marlena. "How?"

Carm answered. "The quarantine is designed to protect you and everyone else beyond those doors. This is a secure facility. It follows regulations set by the feds for biological containment facilities. The public was never expected to be down here. Since the Array has been running, we're all under quarantine for the next twenty-four hours. Unless someone comes walking through that fire door and lets us out."

Terry shrugged. Cracker kicked the wall. "I don't believe this, man. This party's over and I'm for getting out of this joint. If I see that Carl again, I'm gonna kick some hairy-ass butt. And he's damn well gonna spring for something valuable." He sniffed. "At least a six-pack."

Carm looked worried.

"Give Gary the tour, Carmy." Alice was in her stern mode.

Carm heard a pop and glanced at Alice. Yes, she marveled, she still had her gum. Carm let out a breath and put on her tour guide hat. "If Mr. MacDonald has no problem with visitors..."

"But...where is he?"

"He never–"

Alice frowned. She put her hands to her mouth. "Mr. MacDonald!" She peered about. "Nicky!"

Ruben's brows rose and he exchanged silent glances with Carm.

No answer.

"Well, there's nothing we can do now."

"Yeah. Maybe he made it to the Mayor's function. Somehow."

"Yeah. Somehow."

They all looked up. A foreign sound penetrated the low humming of the servers. Behind them the door to the stairwell swung open. A man in brown slacks sloshed in, his shoes squeaking. He smiled.

"Cliff!"

"Don't let the door close–" they yelled.

The door slammed shut.

Cliff turned. "Oops."

Silence.

Melanie turned to Terry. "Next party, Terry–include

me out." She flopped into a canvas work chair.

"Where did you–"

"I hope I didn't pull your collar too hard, Carm. I put you in the elevator with the others and then went back again. When I returned, the elevator had gone and wouldn't come back up." Cliff scratched his head. "I checked every floor trying to find you guys."

"Did you see anyone else? Can they hear us?"

He shook his head. "Building's deserted. We were the last. Everyone is either out of town or underground in shelters." He looked around. "This isn't a bad place to be actually, till the worst blows over. The windows on every floor are blown out."

"Well we got an entire day to wait till it does."

"Oh?"

While Ruben explained, Gary approached a monitor set in the midst of the Array. "I've read about this. I've even filed patents on it. But I've never seen it." Gary looked at Alice, an air of excitement about him.

Alice joined him and ran a finger along one ridge. "Yeah. Well, it's...way cool. And way expensive." She looked to Carm. Bright and happy.

"What's it do?" asked Cliff. "I mean besides dice vegetables and remove unwanted hair like nobody's business."

The others laughed and gathered around Carm.

"You might call it an evolution machine. Or a silicon god, to wax poetic."

Bill shook his hat again and stared, puzzled. Melanie found some lipstick and began putting it on. Gary produced reading glasses and inspected the monitor where a screen-saver with the balding head of Stephen Wolfram was superimposed on the nude torso of a svelte blonde bombshell. Ruben muttered something, touched a key and it vanished.

"You know about genetic transfer technology?" asked Carm.

"Huh?" Bill put his hat on and thumped it for emphasis. "Whassat?"

"Yeah," said Cliff. "I know. It's in all our food. Freeze-resistant genes in our tomatoes. Goats giving silk protein in their milk."

"Bingo. Some sixty percent of what we eat, and growing fast. Well, this does one better. We don't just transfer a gene or two. We produce the whole organism. You see, in cancer research the problem has always been the huge number of parameters involved. In fact, the word cancer is a misnomer since we now know there are hundreds, even thousands of different disorders that we lump under that term. To cure each of these would require its own foundation, its own Institute, its own funding, and so on. That's why there has been so little progress, despite the huge advances in theoretical knowledge."

Cliff shook his head. "Poor Aunt Martha."

"Primal Lab took a different approach." Carm turned. "Cliff, how do you cure a computer virus? I mean one that infects the whole system, a true cancer?"

"Well, hopefully you backed up your system. Then you do a recover to put everything back the way it was before the virus infected it."

"Exactly. You could debug every program one at a time and then scan the drivers to make sure you got every trace, but it's easier and safer to restore the original program, or the entire system, the way it was before it was damaged. That's more sensible than trying to cure every segment individually. Enter genetic programming."

Carm opened a large plastic tray.

"Behold the genechip. One-half of the secret. Most genechips are produced by placing a few strands of genes on a silicon tray and fixing them with repeated dousing of chemical agents. The DNA is either marked with fluorescence or they do their magic by a natural bioelectric negative charge. These are Primal Lab genechips. Each Primal chip has not merely a few strands, but the complete DNA coding of an entire organism, and fixed bioelectrically for access by a computer."

Gary adjusted his glasses and probed among several genechips in the tray with a pencil.

Cliff looked impressed, but skeptical. "So how does that little thing make monsters?"

"That's just an expression. With the exception of a few wolves in accounting, there are no monsters at the Mac-Donald Institute. But we do create life." Carm turned to the monitor and inserted the genechip in an aperture. A red light glowed.

"Now, the other half of the secret. Strange to call it that because it's no secret at all. Conway's Game of Life is on everybody's desktop, and that's all the Array does is play the game."

Bill pushed back his hat. Gary glanced at Alice.

"Damn," said Cliff, "I got that at home! You try to create artificial life based on a few simple rules applied to different initial conditions. Then you sit back and see what happens."

"What you don't have is the most powerful array of redundant computing power in any lab in the world, which controls every nutrient and environmental parameter in a series of aquatic tanks and pools."

"But how can a simple set of DNA produce an animal?"

"Maybe it humps the thing." Cracker turned to Terry and they slapped palms.

"No. You're right," continued Carm. "A few DNA strands can't produce anything. Even if you have a complete sequence. What it can do, however, is translate that chemical sequence into code that a machine can understand and let the machine do it. Once the Array reads the code, it then knows what it wants. The code becomes superfluous." Carm retrieved the genechip and placed it back in the tray. "The genechip can be used many times, but the Array will never need it again. We keep them around only to tell the Array to initiate the process." The nearest blue totem began to hum and was joined domino-fashion by the others.

"Now the Array has a problem. It knows what it wants–the complete gene sequence of a particular organism that it has translated into machine code–but it doesn't know how to make the organism. So it works backwards. It runs a sophisticated version of Conway's Game of Life, testing millions of potential rules, applying them to billions of sets of initial conditions, until it finally stumbles onto the unique combination that will result in the exact gene code that we placed in its memory."

"And then..."

"It runs the algorithm. But finding the right combination takes a while. It's a bit like telling the computer to predict the weather on a particular day a century from now. Even the simplest multi-cellular animals that we began with took weeks of cranking away at full power in order to find the exact evolutionary sequence required to produce them. However, if the Array has already seen the genechip, and already performed the calculations, then the time required is only a fraction of the time it took for its initial run."

Carm pressed Enter on the keyboard. Alice walked down the aisle and Carm followed her. The rest brought up the rear. They approached a massive metal door that could have been borrowed from a submarine but for a thick glass window at eye level. Ruben swung it open and they entered an adjoining warehouse, darker than the fluorescent lab that housed the Array, and larger. A maze of green tanks and pools filled with solution multiplied before them. Carm paused before a small aquarium.

"Bill, put your ear against the glass."

Hesitant, he removed his hat. A moment passed. "Is that...?"

She nodded.

A buzzing, barely audible, emanated from within the tank and rose above them. It sank and Alice slapped her arm. She held it out to reveal a black and red splotch.

"If that don't put the Indian in the gulch."

"A mosquito!"

"And fully grown. The evolution program that the Array discovered was designed to produce this exact mosquito, which is a perfect clone of the original on the genechip, not an egg. Or rather, in this case, it produced a perfect larva that became a mosquito the moment it was created." Carm glanced towards the tank. "We're still restricted by the need to supply liquid nutrients during the process. So we focus on aquatic insects or organisms like mosquitos that begin their life in water. Our next project is aquatic vertebrates–fish."

"Damn, Carm!" said Cliff. "Damn!"

Gary took out a handkerchief and mopped his brow. He stood motionless, staring at the ceiling.

"A billion years of evolution–in one minute."

"But how does that cure cancer?" asked Terry.

"The Array can produce organisms in any stage of development, so duplicating human stem cells will be no problem. We expect to just input that particular genechip when we're ready. Stem cells are aquatic."

"Uh, you lost me."

"Stem cells are what we use to reboot the patient's 'operating system', and restore the healthy initial condition, rather than debugging every tissue and body part separately with harsh chemicals."

"I'll take your word for it, doc."

"Same here. We haven't tested stem cells yet, or any organism more complex than insects."

Terry turned to Melanie. "What do you think of that, Mel? A one-minute mosquito!"

"Like we need more of them." She walked off.

Ed looked at Marlena. A tear formed in her eye.

Chapter 4

"I don't care what you say. I'm telling you I'm gonna sue their ass." Cracker pulled on the metal bar till it gave way. He tossed it aside in disgust and again kicked the fire door.

"Calm down, Cracker. It's only twenty-four hours." Terry washed his wounds with some tap water, then began to re-wrap them in a strap torn from a medical gown in the coat room.

Melanie accepted a Diet Coke from Alice. "Is this all you got?" Reluctantly she gulped it. "It's a fucking conspiracy, I tell you. The Illuminati have nothing over Coke distributors. Just try to get anything else and you'll be visited by the Men in Black at midnight." She lay her languid gaze on Carm and Gary who sat near. "They're really the Coke police. The Board of Directors moonlighting." She shouted. "Will you cut out the crap, Cracker? That door's made of metal in case that hasn't sunk in yet. It's not like you got any place to go."

He strutted before her. "Well maybe I'd just like the choice of not goin' there." He folded his arms and peered about. "I don't like bein' closed in. It's not my thing."

"Yo thang?" Mel laughed. "Well, then just do what you wanna do, jerk."

Cliff turned to Ruben. "Twenty-four hours, you say?"

Ruben nodded. He opened his mouth, paused when he

saw Cracker. The others stared at Cracker until he dropped his gaze. "At least."

Breathing stopped.

"Whadaya mean 'at least'?" asked Gary.

"There have been problems, like with the lights. The security system was originally set up to force a minimum quarantine of twenty-four hours each time the Array manufactured a new batch of organisms. Say, a culture of E.Coli. But then it started triggering the quarantine after *every* new organism."

"How's that?" Cliff asked.

"After we graduated from molds and bacteria to insects, the computer mistook each new insect for a new batch of bacteria, and triggered the quarantine. Ten mosquitos made it lock the door for ten days."

"Ten days!"

"Don't worry. That's when we fixed it. Last winter we had the security system rewired during the building's reconstruction."

Gary sat up. "Wild Bill Construction."

"Maybe," said Ruben. "We instructed the work crew to install a separate timer to override the security system so that no matter what instructions the Array sent, no quarantine would last longer than twenty-four hours for each batch, no matter how many organisms were produced in that batch."

"I get it," said Cliff. "That means the only way you can get locked in here for more than twenty-four hours is if someone inserts another genechip in the Array and makes another animal."

"It must be a different genechip," added Carm. "You can insert the same genechip any number of times without triggering the quarantine. I didn't extend the quarantine when I created the mosquito because we've been working with that genechip for weeks."

"Then why are we here? Why are the doors locked?"

"Well, that's what I said earlier," continued Ruben. "There's a malfunction. For several months now the doors have been locking even though we inserted the same genechip. And sometimes it has lasted for more than twenty-four hours. Even five days."

Cracker spun and kicked the door again. "I don't believe this shit!"

"I gotta have a cigarette," said Melanie, sinking deeper in the chair.

"No can do," said Ruben. "Smoking would contaminate everything."

Carm spoke. "That's when we asked MacDonald to call the architect who designed the reconstruction and get it fixed."

The overhead fluorescents flicked again.

"I think it's the wiring."

A cowboy hat appeared behind some shelving, moving like a target in an arcade game.

"Just the man I wanna see." Cracker picked up an imaginary rifle and started taking potshots. Terry tried the same but winced and let his arm drop.

Bill rounded the corner. "Guys, why so down?"

"You, ya little toad. Ya know what? I think you were takin' a few too many tokes on your weed sticks when you were supposed to be doin' your job last time you were here. And that's why we're in this fuckin' mess."

"I'm sure it's not his fault," said Cliff.

"Yeah? Well, I think I smell another jockey!" Cracker stared at Bill and aimed his finger. "Which means you got a problem!"

Gary looked up from some papers of his that had survived the water. "Cracker may have a point, although his means of expression may not be on a par with most sentient creatures."

Cracker looked puzzled. He dropped his air-gun.

"That may have been an insult, man," said Terry.

"Relax," said Melanie. "He probably didn't know you were sentient when he said that."

Gary continued. "Wild Bill Construction assumed the responsibility for the wiring, and is therefore liable for its faulty operation."

"That's your opinion?" asked Bill.

"And it's a freebie."

"Dude, I explained the problem."

"Then explain it again, toad! Cause we'd like to know why the lights don't work."

"Faulty transformer. There's a spare over there."

The others looked blankly at him.

"And what about this twenty-four hour bit? Why are we stuck?"

"Like I said, podner, the maintenance bo–" he looked at Ruben, "uh, the technicians probably didn't set the timers right."

Carm spoke up. "Could you check?"

"No problemo."

Bill and Carm and Ruben walked to the computer monitor.

"You gotta disengage the security first," said Bill.

Ruben placed his hands over the keyboard, then paused. He stared at the others till they turned their backs. A moment passed. "Done."

Walking to a conduit, Bill read a digital meter. He frowned. "Let's look at the terminusss... terminusesses... terminim. The goldang doors."

They walked to the elevator and Bill glanced at a meter attached to a similar conduit. He frowned. They approached the fire door and Bill repeated his inspection.

"Where are the others?"

"In the tank room."

Passing through the submarine door, they approached a similar door at one corner of the complex of greenish tanks and pools, but which lacked a window.

Bill frowned again. "Where does this lead?"

"Parking garage. For emergencies only."

Cracker stepped forward. "Whadaya call this, asshole, if not an emergency?"

"Enough already, Cracker."

"It's inoperative. Shut permanently when we installed the computer. Only if the Array itself is destroyed could you open it, otherwise you would need a wrecking ball. Like I said, emergencies only."

"Any more doors?" asked Bill.

"No," said Carm.

"Yes there is. One." Ruben pointed. "Remember? The far corner, over there."

They crossed and found another door like the others, complete with glass aperture and rubber seals.

Bill examined the meter.

"Do you have a voltmeter?"

"Sure," said Ruben. He brought one.

Wild Bill peered and probed. He shook his head. "Nope. Nope. Nope. And nope."

"What does that mean?"

"No problemo." He looked up. "They all work fine."

"Oh, man," snorted Cracker. "Like I said, the toad was toked."

"The wiring is fine, dude. So are the meters. The problem is somewhere else." He scratched his head. "I don't savvy it. All I know is them doors should be open."

The others began to drift away.

Bill glanced through the glass window in the metal door. "What's through there, amigo? I see a light."

Ruben shook his head. "Can't." He looked. "Oh, that must be part of the tunnel. But it's unfinished."

The others drifted back.

"Tunnel? What tunnel?"

"I don't really know because I've never been in there." Ruben looked up. An imaginary bulb flashed. "That's right. Our architect mentioned that we were connected to the city's underground tunnel system." He peered through the window again. "I suppose that's it." He shrugged.

"You mean *The* Tunnel?" asked Carm.

"The one and only."

Carm brightened. "Why, that's perfect! We'll just walk right through." Her fingers did a promenade.

"Is it a subway?" asked Gary.

"No," answered Ruben. "There is no transportation in the city tunnel system. Just a complex of underground shops and corridors. You can cross from some buildings in the city to others, entirely underground."

"Yeah," Cliff added. "I been down there. Whatever you want, you can find. It's a whole separate city. There's even a mall. But I haven't been down there in years."

Ed looked at Marlena. She had a strange look about her as if the distant object that she was watching had drawn closer.

"Whoa. Wait a minute," said Cliff. "We're at least a mile from city center. There's nothing but parkland between us and downtown. If this does connect it's gonna be a long walk and may be dangerous."

Carm peered again. "Well that's definitely an electric light I see. And it definitely leads toward town."

"But is it safe?"

"Don't know," answered Ruben. "Several years ago after a storm hit, much of the tunnel flooded, so the city equipped the entire complex with a series of locks. Gate-seals like this. They're designed to close automatically if there's a flood, and compartmentalize the entire system."

"You mean like the Titanic?"

"Something like that."

"Anyway, they're centrally controlled, and, if I remember right, video cameras every hundred feet or so. And supposed to be well lit. Except the bond election failed, so much of it was never finished, including the section you're looking at."

"That's enough for me," said Cliff.

Alice spoke. "Guys, what does it matter? We are still sealed in for at least a day, and probably longer. No one can get past this door."

Ruben pointed to a pull-chain at the top. "Not so. Every door connected to the tunnel has an emergency opener for fail-safe, and an emergency power button to close it manually in the event of a flood. City regs."

"What happened to your federal crap?" asked Melanie.

Ruben shrugged.

Gary took over. "Probably federal grant-matching. That requires local jurisdiction. If you pay, the feds club you to death. But if the feds pay, the city can do almost whatever it pleases." He shrugged too. "Go figure."

Carm removed her lab coat. "I don't know about you guys, but I'm going. Something happened to Carl, and my kids might be stuck, and I'm not staying down here for the next few days without knowing."

The circular crank squealed as Carm wrenched it counter-clockwise. When the crank had been unscrewed, Ruben reached up and yanked the pull-chain. The door popped open spewing dust. To Ruben's horror, a gush of water spilled into the tank room from the tunnel.

"This is a no-go, people. Definitely a no-go. I've got to shut this door now. Step in or step out."

Carm stepped through, followed by Bill, "Well, who's coming with us?" She paused to glance at her watch, was surprised to see that it was already ten o'clock, shocked that it worked at all.

"I'm not staying in this small town one minute longer. Outa my way." Melanie stepped in. Without looking back, she added "Bring the keys, jerk."

Terry took a step and halted–Cracker had his arm. "Hey, man. I ain't goin' through no sewer!"

"The water's dark," said Carm, "but it's not a sewer. And there's fresh air coming from somewhere."

Cliff peered into the gloom. "I don't like this one little bit." He glanced at the stream that already flowed over his shoes. Shaking his head, he followed.

Ed looked even more gloomy. "Nostradamus didn't mention tunnels in his readings."

"You mean Cayce, Ed," replied Marlena. "Nostradamus wrote poetry." They entered.

"Alice?"

"Not me, Carm. I don't even *like* rugrats. You go for it. Ruben and I will cover for you if Boss-man shows up." She smiled showing a mouthful of gum-wrapped teeth. Gary stepped back to keep the spreading pool of water off his luxury loafers.

Cracker put his head through the doorway. He swallowed. Finally he entered the tunnel and slogged to catch up with the others.

"Have fun," called Ruben, and punched the button to close the gateseal. It began to creak shut.

"When we find the mall, what do you want us to bring you?"

"The cash registers…and a soft taco!" The gate slammed shut, its metallic clang echoing past them toward a distant and elusive end.

Chapter 5

Under the lamp, they halted. Bill threw back his hat. "Long-life fluorescent. Shielded with plastic to keep out the humidity. Hasty job." He glanced around. "And a video camera. But it's not hooked up."

"Great. What about an emergency box? There's gotta be an emergency box." Cliff looked around.

"I don't think so," said Carm. "Look how cramped this corridor is. It's too narrow for crowds, and the ceiling is too low for comfort." She shook her head. "And the distance between lights. This section was not intended for the public."

"Well, let's go. I don't want to stay down here any longer than I have to." Melanie set out.

They started to walk, their feet rippling the water ahead and behind to disappear in the surrounding gloom. They came to the next lamp. It flickered uncertainly. Several more passed in a row, separated by long stretches of night. The tunnel angled left, then right, and several smaller passages intersected along one side. A series of rooms appeared, containing debris, then a corridor that turned repeatedly, giving off multiple side-corridors. Coming to a fork, they chose one. Finally, they halted. Ahead was blackness.

Cliff spoke. "Like I said. I don't like this one little bit."

"What do we do?" asked Terry.

"It's not too late to go back."

Melanie pursed her lips. "You're on your own if you do. I'm goin' on."

"Hey, amigos, I just remembered," Bill said smartly. He reached into a pocket of his overalls and withdrew a small flashlight. "I always keep this with me." He turned it on and cast a feeble ray into the darkness.

"Well thank you Jesus we've been saved," snorted Cracker.

Bill ventured ahead, the light glimmering off wires suspended above like exposed roots. "It turns here. There's another fluorescent further up." They followed and paused beneath its narrow patch. Gray water lapped at their shins.

Melanie produced her cigarettes and lit one with a paper match. Inhaling deeply, she funneled the smoke out in a series of O's that rose toward the overhead.

"Do you have to do that?" asked Terry. He dropped his arm and winced, then cradled it with the other.

"Afraid I might turn on the sprinklers?" Ash tumbled into the water. Her eyes followed it down. "I haven't seen my ankles since we entered this place. My feet will never be dry again."

Cracker wiped his brow, "Let's just keep moving. It can't be much further to downtown."

This time Carm led the way while Bill kept the torch directly in front of her. The walls retreated, one side dimly illuminated by the night sky filtering through the hurricane as it beat on several glass panes perched twenty feet above three wide double doors. A steady stream of water poured in around the panes.

"Dammit. They're too high." Terry and Cracker peered into the corners for something to stand on, but soon gave up.

Bill passed the circle of light over the doors. "Hey, these are elevators!"

"Yeah, man. Let's ring for service."

"These elevators are for supplies." Cliff looked up. "We must be beneath the park somewhere. I suppose that's a supply shack above us. One that the hurricane hasn't blown down yet. Well, here goes." Cliff pressed the only button. For a moment a grinding sounded as the carriages began to move, then sparks flashed and all three jerked to a halt. Smoke drifted from behind the panel.

"If that don't beat all," said Bill.

"I don't believe this!" Cracker yelled. He and Terry rushed forward and kicked the elevators, soon covering each door with scuff-marks.

Mel gazed at Carm. "Who needs brains when you got a good strong boot?" She lit another cigarette with the end of her first.

Bill aimed the flashlight and resumed walking. Cliff shrugged and joined him, and the others followed.

Blank gray walls ran along either side, devoid of life. After several more turns, the walls ended abruptly in a metal barrier.

"Hey, look at this. Must be another one of them gate-seals Ruben talked about." Cliff ran his hand along the rubber perimeter.

"Locked, right?" said Bill. "They're supposed to lock automatically when water gets in here. Spring-loaded or somethin'." He looked around. "I suppose that's why the water isn't over our heads."

"Yeah, but it's getting in anyhow. They didn't plan for the mother of all hurricanes."

They took turns peering through the glass window.

"Can't see much."

"No, but there's a couple more lights ahead. Let's pull the chain."

Cracker helped Terry lean against one wall. "Wait," said Terry. "Are you sure this is a good idea? I mean, what if the water on the other side of that door is higher than in here?"

Cliff shook his head. "It's not by much. We can see it from the window."

Terry exhaled. "If you're sure."

Cliff took hold of the chain and pulled. With a bang the door popped open and a torrent of water bowled them over. The door creaked and slammed against the wall.

"Great!" exclaimed Terry, inspecting new bruises on his arm.

Bill stood. "If that don't put the hog in the trough. This dang water is all over my overalls now. And that's the end of my hat." He flung it aside.

"Sorry," said Cliff. "That could have been better."

Carm shook her head. "Couldn't be helped."

Mel stared at the water. The flow rushed past them for a minute then began to ease. "Meathead was right. This level is higher. Or was."

Terry smiled at his promotion from asshole.

"Must be another gate ahead."

"But what if the water behind the next gate is higher than this was?" asked Bill.

Cracker snorted. "Well, we'll just have to deal with that when we get there, won't we toad?"

They pressed forward and entered a low, wide chamber. Assorted construction gear lay stacked about, thrusting from the water like miniature oil platforms.

"Shouldn't we shut the other door?" asked Terry.

"What for? That'll just block all the water in here with us. Not a good idea. Better to leave it open in case we have a problem later."

Threading a patch through the equipment, they halted. On the far side of the chamber a half dozen apertures beckoned. All were narrower and more cramped than the one they had exited.

"Will you guys stop stopping and get going?" called Melanie. "City center is this way–" She tossed the stub of her cigarette and headed for one of the center apertures.

"The hell you say. There ain't even a light in that one."

Carm peered ahead. She took several steps then returned. "Terry's right. This one curves, but it seems to go in the right direction."

They followed Carm, clustering more closely around Bill's light as the silence and the blackness grew more complete.

They threaded several more corridors, then Cliff turned to Carm. "Didn't know you had kids. Otherwise, I wouldn't have said what I did."

"You were right. I don't know what I was thinking when I agreed to work late. I saw the weather report; I should have known."

"But your husband–"

"Died two years ago. I've been a single parent since." Carm paused. "I mean, until I met Carl."

"Who?"

"My new husband. Didn't he invite you? This was his idea of a hurricane party."

Cliff shook his head. "Like I said, I just wandered in off the street. Someone mentioned free beer, and there I was." He glanced above them again. "Looks like I'll never see my Aunt Martha again."

"You're right," said Ed. "But it's the other way around. She'll never see you again. Or any of us." Ed slowly shook his head, peering deeply into the gloom.

Cliff halted. "Listen," said Cliff. "What do you hear?" They all stopped to listen.

"Nothin'. I don't hear the storm. Or nothin'."

"You won't," said Ed. He passed his round owl-eyes over them. "Don't you know where we are? Even in ancient times they knew better than to go underground without charms or incantations. We've entered the spirit world." Ed stared ahead to the next sullen glow. "There are ghosts down here. Marlena knows when someone has entered the spirit world, the strange way they walk. After a time you can see right through them. That'll be us if we don't get out of here soon."

Cracker rubbed sweat off his palms, and blinked. "Man, I don't need this. Do you think you can shut the fuck up?"

"Let's just go, can we?" Carm caught up to Bill, and the others hurried to join.

They followed the corridor around several more bends. More side passages opened beside them, gaping as if daring them to enter. After what seemed a great length of time they entered a wide, low room piled high with construction gear. On the far side, a half dozen cramped apertures beckoned.

"Which way?" asked Cliff. He looked at Carm.

Carm looked at Bill. "The flashlight is going out."

Bill looked around in silence, passing the now rapidly dimming ray over the gear and equipment. "You know what?"

"No..."

"Don't say it."

"We're turned around. This is the same goldang room we passed through a while ago."

"Yep, we're lost."

"Damn!" said Cliff. "Why does this always happen?"

The others looked at him strangely.

Cracker exploded. "You've gotta be fucking kidding." He rubbed his palms again. "Well ain't that just dandy?" He turned to Bill. "You know somethin? This is your fuckin' fault. Why don't you look in them Farmer Brown pockets of yours, toad, for something else to help us, like maybe a compass." He strained to catch his breath.

"I only wish I had one, pal. Maybe there's one among all this shit them hardhats left behind."

"Hey, that's not a bad idea," said Cliff. "Maybe there's a map in here somewhere, a map of the tunnels."

"Spread out, see what you can find." They began picking among the boxes.

Carm called out, "I can't see anything. Any luck with you?"

"No."

"Shit!" A pile of gear crashed into the water. Splashing sounded, followed by a gurgle.

"What was that? Bill, where's the light?"

"If that don't beat all," yelled Terry. "I just fell over something. I think I hurt my leg."

A sudden beeping startled them. A green light approached, floating through the air.

"What did I tell you?" called Ed. "It's the spirits! They're coming!"

They panicked till Bill appeared, holding a cell phone. "Yeah, podner, it's the ghost of AT&T. Who wants to make the first call?" He grinned. "And," he produced an electric work-light, "courtesy of your friend and mine, the Mayor."

They sighed in relief.

"Damn, Wild Bill," said Cliff. "That's great! But hand the phone to Carm so she can call her kids."

"Thanks." She took it. Slowly she pressed the buttons, and pressed Send.

"It won't work. We're too far underground. It needs an open window."

"Not always. Besides we can search for a pipe to use as an antenna."

"If you think you can find a dry one."

Mel sloshed over to Terry. "Let me see your leg." Bill shined the light. "Yep, you're bleeding. You need a doctor. You're a mess."

Cracker stepped close to the phone. "Hold it, man. Terry needs a doctor. We're makin' the first call."

"Slow down, she's already dialed."

"Nothin' doin'. Hand it over!"

Carm whooped. "It's ringing!" She jumped, raising a splash. "I've got the daycare! Hello? Hi, Mary, this is Carmen Niles calling for Cheyenne and Burke. Can you tell me..."

The others could hear a voice emanating from the speaker, punctuated by static, "–I've stepped away from my desk, please leave your name and number."

Cliff and Bill slowly shook their heads.

Carm put her free hand to her forehead to concentrate. She shut her eyes. "Mary, sorry I missed you, this is Ms. Niles calling. We were rained in at work. And I'm underground in the tunnel system. I'm on my way to get Cheyenne and Burke, but we're having a little trouble and we may be late–"

"That's enough, doc lady." Cracker snatched the phone and hit the End button. "Terry's next."

"What the–?" Bill and Cliff grabbed Cracker by either arm and pulled him back. The phone hit the water and went under.

Everyone groaned.

"Sonofabitch! Look what ya did now." They let him go and Cracker glared at them and Carm. "Ya know, I'd expect this from Farmer Brown, but you done sneaked up on me. Man, what a life. If it ain't camel jockeys, it's friggin' jungle bunnies! We coulda got some help and some directions instead of messing with some damn kids!" He kicked another stack of gear, which fell clattering into the sink.

"Just calm down."

"Cracker, you didn't have to do that," said Mel.

"The hell I didn't."

Cracker and Melanie retreated, arguing.

Cliff turned to Carm. "'We're having a little trouble and we may be late'?" His brows lifted.

She shrugged. "If you don't let them know, they charge a dollar a minute."

"Oh." That explained everything.

A moan distracted them. "I don't feel so good."

Melanie and Cracker returned. "There's something wrong with Terry. I think he broke his leg. And his wounds look worse. This water. It's not good."

They quieted and gathered around. Locating a steel span, they tied it to his leg for a splint. Another length served as a crutch. Terry sat on some debris and raised his feet out of the water. He quietly groaned.

They sat and rested, turning the lamp off to save power. The darkness affected them more than before, slowly pressing in on them like a great weight.

Several minutes passed. Carm looked up. "Listen again," she whispered. "This time I definitely heard something."

"Yeah, like something slapping the surface."

Bill switched on the lamp, which shone in the darkness like a full moon.

"Maybe it's ghost beavers." The others looked at Cliff. He smiled. "I read about them in the Enquirer."

Behind him, Ed looked at Marlena and trembled. Her eyes were wide as in a trance and her skin was ashen-gray.

Chapter 6

The lift rang and Carl exited the elevator. The smell of exhaust enveloped him and he noted with disgust that a layer of grime and dust had already settled on his new leather jacket. Several automobiles occupied scattered spaces in the parking garage. Far fewer than usual. Most were bumper to snout on the interstate trying to escape the hurricane. He nodded with relief–and wished that even fewer were present. For his next rendezvous, he wished no witnesses.

With any luck, his visitors would not show. He had kept his promise, the party was under way, and he had been well paid; moreover, his side business had been eminently successful. He was flush with cash. If his creditors failed to keep their appointment to claim their money, that would be their bad luck. Should they miss their date, the spreading lake under some of the cars supplied him with a perfect pretext to skip town.

A rumbling of motors deflated his hopes. Three Harleys and a four-door pickup surrounded his suburban. He hesitated. Riding shotgun was Ray. As Carl resumed his approach, Ray watched without blinking.

"Ray. Glad you could make it. I was afraid the hurricane might have held you up." Carl nodded to the others. "Cole. Dicker. Griff." Two more sat in the truck. Carl searched for signs of trouble in the tone of voice and in their eyes–as if the 'Grapplers' logo on their club jackets was not trouble enough.

Ray continued to stare. A minute passed and Carl began to wonder if he had misread the signs and could expect his imminent demise, but he recalled the purpose of their visit and calmed. Without him, they could not collect. He waited patiently, hands in pockets.

"Get your hands out of your pockets, Carl."

Surprised, he complied.

Ray looked at Dicker and he revved his hog behind Carl. Both barrels of a shotgun contacted the back of Carl's head.

"You know, Carl, I've been sittin' here tryin' to think of what I was gonna say so that you could understand me better."

"Yeah, Ray?"

"Yeah, boot-breath. You see, I don't think you understand me well. In fact, I don't think you understand me at all."

"Ray, I explained last week–"

"What? What was that?" Ray leaned out of the truck and pinched Carl's nose between knuckles. "I don't recognize that word, pretty boy. In fact, it's obvious that you don't understand shit!"

Griff lit a cigarette and handed it to Cole. He took a drag and gave it to Ray. After Ray puffed, he looked again at Carl.

"Now, let's see if I have the facts of our situation

right."

Carl nodded, the pain from the fist in his face growing. The shotgun pressed closer.

"Last month you came to me and took delivery on credit of a certain amount of Christmas cheer. In front of me and the boys you put your hand on our clubhouse table, and when I gave you the snow, Dicker tattooed a box on the palm of your hand, which was your invoice. And you said that was okay cause you knew you'd have no problem sellin' my stuff to all your primo highfalutin' contacts. Now, in our good graces, we let you walk off with enough snow to bury half of Chicago three feet deep. And you know what? We still ain't been paid."

"Ray, buddy, you god nuttin' to worry bout. I god de dough!"

"Oh, I hope you're right! Because with interest and our collection fees the amount you owe us is now twice what it was before. And if you don't come through pronto, *you* are gonna owe *us* fucking Fort Knox. And last I heard, you don't *own* fucking Fort Knox."

Ray took another drag. "After thinking about our little problem, though, I've decided that the best thing would be not to waste my breath, pretty boy, but to let your eyes do the talking." He released Carl's nose.

Carl rubbed it, taking care not to jiggle the shotgun.

Ray handed the cigarette to Dicker, who took his entire hand.

With a shock, Carl realized that they passed around

not just a cigarette, but a severed hand with a cigarette planted between two stiff fingers. On the palm was a tattoo of a box.

Carl took a deep breath.

"Yeah, pretty boy. Jose was late with the rent just like you. Now he picks his nose and wipes his ass with the same hand. I trust that we understand each other better now." He glanced behind. "What do you think, Cole? Do you think he understands us better?"

Cole leaned over. Growling, he snapped the rail guides off the roof of Carl's suburban and twisted them into a pretzel.

"Now get in the truck, jackass. You're takin' us to your bank." Ray looked over his shoulder. "Move over, Jimbo. He's gettin' in back with you."

Carl heard the hammers release and Dicker lowered the shotgun. Jimbo opened the door for Carl, and, after he sat, Griff kicked the door shut. The hogs revved, filling the garage with noise.

At the garage exit, they paused, rain hitting the windshield in torrents. The garage was filling with water.

Jimbo produced a .045 pistol, and Ray turned to look at Carl. "Which way, pretty boy? And hey–" He grabbed Carl again, this time by his chin. "This better not be no bank check. Cause all the banks are closed, and we got better things to do than hang around here takin' a goddam bath."

"Don't worry, Ray. Cold hard cash, just like you said.

It's in an exercise locker below the Bank Emporia, at Sweats-R-Us. See? I got the key." Carl rubbed his nose.

Ray snatched the key and grinned. "Just the same, you're comin' along for the ride, in case it ain't there. And, ooo little man, I don't want to even think about what will happen to you if it's not there."

Carl said nothing but lowered his eyes.

Ray peered at the darkening sky. The rain was coming in broad sheets and the avenue beside the Cancer Research Institute already showed more lake than asphalt. "Downtown, Leroy."

Leroy paused. "It's gettin' mighty wet, Ray. What about the hogs?"

"They'll make it. I want that dough tonight. Pedal to the metal."

The truck sped off. Protected from the rain by goggles and helmets, Cole and Dicker and Griff followed on the hogs.

A frustrating hour or so later, after many detours around high water, they finally arrived within a block of the Bank Emporia. A low spot in the road had turned into a river. On one side was a raised sidewalk. On the other, lettering that read: Office of Transportation & Tunnel Services. Above, an old bomb shelter sign had been superseded by a modern neon version. 'Shelters Open' flashed yellow through the black storm.

The truck died. Repeated attempts by Leroy to restart the engine produced only dull clicks. The hogs paused alongside on the sidewalk.

"What are ya doin', Leroy? Let's go."

"It's dead, Ray."

"Jerk. You ain't turnin' the key right. Don't you know how to drive a truck?"

"It's the water. Look at all the stalled cars. It's got us, too."

"Move over. Out of my way."

Leroy opened the door and water poured inside.

"Goddamn it!" Ray kicked at Leroy. "You soaked me, you moron! Gimme the key!" Ray struggled with the engine, flooring the pedal.

Carl looked up. The fourteen-story Bank Emporia building rose ahead. Even at the distance of a city block, he could hear the storm blowing its windows in with audible pops. The few remaining occupants would be headed underground to the tunnels, and the street was empty but for several abandoned vehicles increasingly obscured by the downpour.

He looked askance at Jimbo. Like Ray, he was engrossed with the engine. His right hand held the gun slackly, his finger off the trigger.

Carl cracked his door. Gripping Jimbo's right hand in his, he daggered an elbow into Jimbo's jaw. Something crunched. Jimbo dropped the gun, and Carl snapped it up. Kicking the door wide, Carl stood on the seat and clambered into the truck bed.

While Ray's head bobbed up in confusion, Dicker,

Griff and Cole spun their bikes round in an attempt to reverse direction. Carl turned and ran toward the Emporia Bank, leaving them facing the wrong way.

Cole tried to reverse again, but skidded into Dicker and Griff. They halted.

Leaping out, Ray watched Carl melt into the night.

"Aaah!" He banged his fist on the hood. He motioned for Jimbo and Leroy to climb behind Griff and Cole, then jumped behind Dicker. "What are you waiting for? Directions?"

The bikes stabilized. With a terrific roar, the three hogs jerked in pursuit. Rumbling down the sidewalk to avoid the swamp in the street, they raced to the Emporia.

Without warning, the Harleys burst into the lobby. People screamed. Those too slow to leap aside were run down as the hogs traced eights amid belching smoke.

Ray pointed to the down escalator, and grinned. "Let's get us some exercise!" he yelled over the roar of the motors.

Dicker nodded. He steered his hog onto the steps, revved and sped down triggering a stampede among the pedestrians. Cole and Griff followed. They emerged in a brightly lit, well-maintained section of the tunnel, which was entirely dry, and the bikers raced ahead. An open ten-foot gateseal appeared. They sped through, tires bucking at the threshold to spin air.

Moments later they sighted a garish sign: 'Sweats-R-Us." Slowing, they cut off the engines and rolled forward in silence.

Behind the counter a metallic sound reverberated as if a length of pipe had fallen. Carl backed out, mumbling.

Griff rolled near and Jimbo slipped off.

"Gotcha!" Jimbo grabbed Carl by his collar.

Ray dismounted from behind Dicker. "Yeah, asshole! Guess who? My, are you in deep shit now. Cause now we're gonna take your money, and whatever snow you still got, and your nose-picker. When we get through with you, pretty boy, you won't be shakin' hands with no more pals, and you won't be porkin' no more pretty ladies–unless they like real ugly one-armed guys with no money! How do you like that, Mr. Postman?"

From his pocket, Carl drew Jimbo's 045.

Everyone froze.

As in slow motion, the barrel aimed and fired twice. "Shit!"

Ray and Leroy ducked. Cole lay over his bike, which did a three-sixty. Dicker wheelied around a corner while Jimbo lurched back and dropped his eyes to a red stream that erupted from his chest.

Griff slipped off his bike. Falling to the ground with a thud, he released it, and Carl, steadying the bike by a handlebar, hopped into the seat. Without a backward glance, he revved down the corridor.

"He shot me, Ray," Jimbo blurted. The others stared in shock as Jimbo sat heavily and let his hands fall to the floor.

Ray helped Cole lift his Harley back up. Griff propped himself on one elbow. He winced. "He got me in the rib." Blood from the second bullet flowed from a gash in his side.

Dicker reappeared. "Go get him! Now!" Ray jammed his finger in Carl's direction. With a deafening roar, Dicker revved up. Reaching behind, he pulled out his shotgun and propped it on his hip. His front wheel rose; the back wheel churned. He lurched in pursuit.

Jimbo was dead. While Leroy stared, Cole and Ray stepped behind the counter. Here were two rows of key-opened exercise lockers.

"What's the number on the key?"

"Two twenty-one."

Ray found two twenty-one and opened it.

"How much money he got in there, Ray? I need a new pair of shoes, and my old lady, too."

"Nothin."

"Huh?"

Ray held up a pair of women's tennis shoes. "Nothin." He pulled out a single photo. It was a wedding photo of Carl with a woman and two children. "Pretty boy lied."

Within seconds Dicker sighted Carl. His bearded face twisted in triumph as he watched Carl slow, then stop. Without slowing, Dicker cocked both barrels. His eyes widened. Carl had punched the emergency button–the gateseal was closing.

"Son of a bitch!" Dicker took aim. Fired. The first

shot bounced off the metal door, ricocheting in all directions. He fired again. Fragments penetrated the aperture between gate and seal. The rest ricocheted.

"Beer drinkin' dickers and old lady lickers!" Dicker accelerated for all he was worth in a final effort to slip through before the gate sealed shut.

Too late.

Slamming on the brakes, he lost control just as the gate shut with a metallic clang. Bike and Dicker exploded in a fiery ruin.

Down the tunnel, Ray narrowed his eyes. "I'm gonna find that insect if I have to look under every brick in town." He turned to Cole and handed him the photo. "C'mere. I've got a special job for you."

Alice reordered the stack of documents on the table before her. Out of the corner of her eye she watched Ruben finish cleaning the floors in the Lab and cross to the Array's monitor. Soon he was engrossed with routine maintenance of the servers. Alice looked at Gary.

He returned her glance. Casually she entered the coat room. Pausing to turn his jacket over so that the other side would dry atop the Array's exhaust, he too strolled to the coat room. With a last look to check on Ruben, he closed the door behind him.

Alice grabbed Gary and planted a passionate hot kiss. At last she let him go and he fell backwards into a chair. "So what do we do, honey?" Alice wore her stern face, but managed to look earnest.

"Don't worry. Whether they make it out or return to the Lab, we have accomplished our purpose."

"But if they escape, then our plan fails, and all our efforts were for nothing."

"Not necessarily." He stared into her eyes. "Alicia, my darling, all we wanted was to embarrass Nicholas Mac-Donald and the Institute. Carl did what we hired him for by inviting a bunch of losers to a simple hurricane party. We had planned on tricking them into entering the Lab, but the storm did it for us just like it's driving people into shelters all over the city. Now all we need to do is keep them out of circulation till past noon tomorrow. That's when MacDonald's deal with Primal Lab is supposed to be signed. And when they hear that a malfunction kept their inspector–yours truly–imprisoned overnight, along with a dozen disinterested party-goers as witnesses, Primal will kill the deal."

"Don't you think a nice accident or two would help? Think of the headlines: 'MacDonald Cancer Lab malfunctions killing several.'"

Gary laughed. "Your ambition always did have a lethal side, my dear. But this headline works just as well: 'Lawyer envoy trapped overnight–gives thumbs down to Primal deal'."

"But how does that help us?"

"In two ways: First, on my recommendation every partner in my law firm has their brother-in-law massively shorting Primal Lab's stock. When they hear tomorrow that I was held incommunicado at the Institute due to a malfunction, and with witnesses to back me up, that will end the deal, and Primal's stock will crater. Second, when that happens we stop selling and start buying. Once we have control of Primal, we take over its Board of Directors, sue the MacDonald Institute for breach of contract, force a hostile take-over, eject 'Nicky,' and switch the focus of Array research away from cancer to cloning poultry to sell to corporations. By then we won't just be saying 'Hello Rio'–we'll be able to buy Brazil."

The bright happy look returned. Alice nodded fervently, caught up in the pep-talk. She grabbed Gary and kissed him again. Finally he disengaged her arms.

"Now act casual. The last thing we need is for *Rube* to get suspicious and decide to testify at an indictment. Things are under control. Just relax." Gary straightened his shirt and tied his tie, smoothing his hair in the mirror.

Alice smiled beatifically at him.

He winked at her. "That's right, gorgeous. Just keep showing that million dollar smile!" Gary returned to drying his jacket.

Standing by the door, Alice watched in silence. Slowly the stern face returned and for a time she remained motionless. Her gaze wandered to Ruben, still preoccupied with the computer, and her lips compressed and she nodded to herself.

At length, Ruben ceased tending the Array and prepared to bed down for the night. Switching most of the overheads off, he threw some spare clothing and blankets onto a cot in a practiced routine, and Gary and Alice set up similar beds not far from him.

The last of the overheads switched off. Darkness settled, broken by a constellation of red points that burned to the quiet soughing of silicon.

Time passed. A shadow grew over the monitor. Without warning a metal pipe thudded and the shadow let loose a dull cry and collapsed. A second shadow appeared. Drawing a genechip from a pocket, it read the label *Serrasalsus Hollandi*, and inserted the genechip into the Array. Entering the tank room, the shadow inspected a large empty pool, and passed to the gate leading to the tunnel. It turned the crank. With a rush, water spilled into the chamber–more than before. Hurrying from the tank room to the Lab, it sealed the door between them. The humming of the servers quickly gathered strength.

Chapter 7

The slapping sounded again, but closer.

Cliff turned to Bill and Carm. "There couldn't be any-thing... alive down here, could there be?"

They shook their heads.

"No way."

"Right on. I mean, what would it eat?"

"If it lived on fear-tinged sweat, it'd be pretty well fed."

Ed spoke. "All sorts of things live in deep dark places. Everyone knows that. But nothing you want to meet."

Bill shined the beam of the lamp in a circle about them. They moved together for comfort. The surface grew still. From somewhere came a muffled sound of falling water.

"What's that?" They jerked upright.

Bill shined the light on a black smudge that left a wake. The wake widened to cross the other wakes. A lump appeared. The light moved and more lumps sur-faced.

A scream erupted followed by a torrent of squeaks as the lumps emerged from the water to scramble atop the stacks of equipment.

"Get em off!" screamed Terry. Frantically he shook loose a dozen rats and stood on his one good leg, splash-ing at them with his impromptu crutch.

"Cripes! Look at em all!" shouted Cracker.

Melanie and Carm shrieked and froze, instinct telling them to climb up the stacks of gear, but the horde of rats beating them to it.

"I don't know which way is out but I'm making one." Ed waved at them and they ran. Mel and Cracker brought up the rear with Terry.

They found themselves in another poorly lit hallway. The hall angled once. Twice. A flotilla of boxes was jammed in between and they broke it up as they passed through. The current took the boxes back the way they had come, while they entered a wider room.

Mel screamed.

In front of them a large outline rose up. Emerging from the darkness, it shouted in triumph and displayed a rat impaled on a pole.

"My god," said Carm. "That's a man."

"Hey, you!"

The man spun around. For a moment they glimpsed a scraggled unwashed beard framing eyes wide with fear. Then darkness swallowed him.

"Damn. Watch out!"

Cliff stumbled into Bill, sending the lamp into the water and plunging them again in darkness.

"Follow him! Don't let him get away!" The others pushed through the water as fast as their legs could stilt and soon they came to another gateseal, swung wide, marking the end of the compartment. Their pursuit slowed, not only due to Terry whose weight burdened Cracker, but to the fact that the current was stronger and more focused at the threshold. With some difficulty they pushed through.

Cliff paused. "Tell me my eyes deceive me."

The others joined him. "Your eyes deceive you. Mine see truth."

A dozen men and women in torn and stained clothing stood before them, each with a bottle of liquor in one hand, and a spear-like poker in the other. The scraggled fugitive mingled with them. In quick succession they impaled several more rats and tossed their carcasses onto a gradually sloping dais that paralleled a wall along the left. The slope was strewn with rats. One man roasted several on flaming cans of Sterno set around a genuine mesquite wood fire piled on a portable metal table. A broad, thin stream of water flowed from a dozen vents behind the dais to add their bulk to the lake that filled the corridor, some thirty feet in width. Two hundred feet ahead was the next submarine door with glass window. Several of the overheads cast a steady glow, brighter than before, for once illuminating the entire chamber.

Bill and Cliff sloshed toward the nearest drunk, glancing nervously behind them.

"Uh... good hunting?"

"Couldn't be better. Nothing like a little water to make these suckers run." He let a dull glare fall on them, and frowned. "You're not from down here." He slugged a drink. "Who are you? No one invited you. We're having a party–and it's private!" He leaned close and exhaled his nauseous breath.

"What do they want, George?" asked a female companion, shriveled from decades of harsh living.

"Who the fuck cares. They're from up there," he rolled his eyes toward the ceiling. "I can tell from their clothes." He staggered to Carm and pushed into her face. "Up there," he sneered, "where they talk together–eat together–white tie and tails together. And never got no time or a lousy buck for people like us."

"We don't want to bother you, we just want to know the way out."

"Just go through–"

"Shaddup, Juney!" George turned to Carm again, and burped. "You wanna know the way out? Six feet under! Ain't no other way out, no way, no how. That's what you people taught me in your world."

George speared another rat with surprising accuracy. He flung it onto the slope where the blood blended darkly with the water from a hundred small bodies. "This is my world, girlie. Six feet under." He lay a finger by his eye. "And I see right through you."

Carm looked stricken. Bill and Cliff took her by the arms and clambered onto a clean section of the dais, beyond the butchery and the stink. The shallow flow of the water was a relief compared to the ever deepening lake. They sat and exhaled. The fatigue of constantly struggling through the water was beginning to tell.

Cracker helped Terry hobble toward the dais, but paused to adjust Terry's splint.

The band of drunks speared more rats as the number coming through the lock increased. Belting out a drunken limerick, George thrust into the water and once again hit pay dirt. He pulled out the stick to inspect his trophy. "Free drinks for all!" he roared. "I got me a red snapper!"

The fish flapped. Dropping the bottle, he steadied his catch with a hand, then jerked it back. A stump had replaced his finger. Dull pain rushed up nerves to signal something out of sorts with his legs and he stared down to see a cloud of silver blurs burrowing in.

With a grunt like a rhino he went under.

"George?!" Juney tucked her bottle under one arm and attempted to part the water with her hands. She yanked them out and gasped at a string of fish that clung to her flesh, like ornaments.

Screams erupted. In rapid succession each tunnel-dweller collapsed in a bloody welter, a savage tumult marking the spot where he or she had stood.

Dumb-struck, the others stared, unable to move. Carm glanced at the slaughterhouse on the slope. She leaped to her feet. As Cliff and Bill did the same, a phalanx of pretty baubles wriggled up the ramp and began to gnaw the carcasses, encountering no difficulty from the current. The attack came so swiftly that the cook still had a roasted rat in his mouth when the first baubles bit into his gore-soaked shoes. He slipped and slid into the lake. In another moment, only his head remained above the churning water, his teeth clenching his last meal.

The blurs edged down the slope and Carm, Bill, and Cliff half-slid, half-leaped upstream, towards the next gateseal. Marlena and Ed were already there, yanking the pull-chain. The door popped open to release another watery torrent.

"Melanie!" Terry screamed. Terry leaned heavily on Cracker, and Melanie hesitated, closer to the door than they. She paused, then reluctantly went back and helped Cracker pull Terry through the door. Pounding the button, Bill and Cliff stepped aside till the door closed again. Ignoring the stream of escaping rats, they hooked the pull-chain back in place.

Their chests heaved.

"Jesus of all creation! What the *hell* was that?"

They stared through the glass in the door at the maelstrom that consumed the other chamber.

Ed trembled. "It's what I said. It's our fate, our karma. You can't change it. Nobody can." He shook his head. "We'll never get out of here alive."

"It's some kind of fish. But where the hell did they come from?" said Cliff. "And how come we didn't see them before? Man, that was close!"

Carm shook her head, turned and fell back against the door. "*Serrasalsus Hollandi.*"

"Huh? What's that?"

"Piranhas! But how–"

A thump sounded on the other side of the door. Carm jumped and Melanie peered through the aperture–she shrieked and jerked back. George's face slammed onto the glass, more skull than flesh. Bloody hands scraped the glass, the eyes glaring drunkenly at them. 'My world,' the jaws mouthed. He collapsed.

Mel held her heart. "This ain't happenin'. This just ain't happenin' to me." She started off. "I'm outa here. Piranhas? Down here? This can't be happenin'. This ain't real!" She began to run.

"Mel, baby, wait! Wait for me." Terry hobbled after.

The others turned.

"I'll be damned."

Before them was a raised circular garden beside a wide storefront consisting of a glass facade, several of whose panes had been recently smashed. A sign on the storefront read Rick's Liquor. Half empty shelves were visible inside. In the garden, bizarrely, a fountain sprayed, shooting inward from a perimeter of a circle of bricks to cascade in the center. A patch of fluorescent lights set in a ceiling higher than the previous sections threw their dull light over the scene. Beyond the fountain, darkness swallowed Melanie.

The water level was only a little higher than in the previous chamber, and Cliff had no problem pushing his way to the garden where a small spot of gravel sprouting artificial plants offered a dry refuge. Although Carm and

Bill found the water up to their thighs, they soon joined him. Ed and Marlena were next. Terry stumbled forward, assisted by Cracker.

"Mel, come back!" Carm halted. She looked at the others. "Do you hear that?"

Bill nodded. "Sounds like rapids."

They peered to the right of the locked gate. A torrent of water disappeared into a series of gaps just like the apertures in the previous chamber. A further torrent flowed in from some vent overhead.

"I don't think–"

"Maybe we should–"

A blur of silver jewels materialized from the apertures moving with the purpose of a single entity.

"I thought them dang doors compartmentalized this place."

"Our tax dollars at work."

"Terry! Cracker! Run! Get back! They're piranhas!"

Suddenly Cracker and Terry understood and caught their breath.

"It's his blood!" yelled Bill. "They're following the trail from Terry's wounds!"

"Get him outa there!"

"Take him in! Get him out of the water!"

"Run for it! *Run!*"

Cracker halted. He paused to listen, fear drenching his temple. Reaching out, he swung open one of the glass doors to Rick's.

Terry staggered forward a step. "We can make it–"

An arm held him back. "Not in here, man," blurted Cracker. "Your arms…your leg! They smell your blood, man. You're not comin' in here cause then they're comin' in here after you and then they're comin' in here after me!"

"Buddy–"

Cracker shoved Terry back.

Terry slipped to one knee. "Cracker! Help me!"

The glass door shut.

Terry reached for the handle. "*Cracker!!*"

Pressing his face and shoulder against the glass to make certain it did not open, Cracker watched in horror as the cloud surrounded Terry.

Terry took one short breath. Bubbling spumed from below. He shrieked and began to spin slowly round in a blanket of red froth. A minute passed and his clothing floated on the surface, rippling like a bag of snakes. Soon only a skull stared, and a skeletal hand still reaching for safety.

Gray as a corpse, Cracker lurched back. He glanced down. A red tide was flowing in under the glass. Terry's blood. He attempted to stem the flow with his hands; it flowed around them. He moved away from the glass, looked to either side, sighted the broken panes where the water flowed freely. He reached for a box–anything to block the openings.

He failed.

FRENZY

The silver jewels sped through with the inevitability of judgment day searching out every possible harbor.

Beating at them with his fists, Cracker retreated to the shelves. Desperately, he climbed and managed through strength and nimbleness to clear his feet–the shelves began to rip from the ceiling. Creaking loudly, the shelving did a slow dive. Somehow he managed to keep his grip on the highest shelf, but the structure slipped further and Cracker's fingers began to slip, his feet to graze the water.

Like a grinder, the myriad fish snapped in a frenzy just below. One nicked his boot. Another connected. Then more.

Cracker let out a groan.

His fingers slipped to the edge. A crowd of wriggling pearls razored into him, quickly penetrating. From the fountain, the others glimpsed one last sorrowful glance, one last stream of sweat. With a crash Cracker went under, the maelstrom that ensued so ferocious that crimson splashed half the length of the glass doors and a femur bounced off one of the panes to crack it.

Bill looked down. The water level was now even with the bricks. In another minute it would cover the garden. "Dudes, we don't need to be here."

"You got that right."

"Is there any blood on you?" Cliff stared at the others.

They all shook their heads.

"Let's go."

As one, they slipped into the current and plunged into

the darkness where they had last seen Melanie. They soon found an open gateseal, water pouring outward into a section considerably less flooded than the section with the garden.

Ed shouted. "Here they come!"

They splashed through, and Ed punched the button. With agonizing slowness, the door swung. It creaked and halted. Silver bullets shot in their direction at blazing speed. With a jerk, the door resumed and clanged shut just in time–a swarm of silvery fish flashed red bellies as they searched hungrily for a passage.

Chapter 8

"It's my turn." The tow-headed girl of ten in fluffy summer dress selected a piece with care and inserted it in the puzzle. She pulled a tissue free, dabbed a delicate up-turned nose, and tapped the piece into place. "There. That completes Asia. I get a hundred points."

"Not so fast, Cheyenne." A boy with tousled auburn hair. "That's New Guinea. It's not part of Asia. It's part of Oceania. You only get ten."

"Of course it's part of Asia, silly Burke. See? The other half is in Indonesia, which everyone knows is part of Southeast Asia. And it's called Papua New Guinea, not 'New Guinea'."

"Yes, but your piece includes the Solomon Islands and New Caledonia. And everyone knows the Solomon Islands are *not* part of Southeast Asia. They go with Oceania."

Cheyenne rolled her eyes. "You're not seriously telling me that New Caledonia goes with Oceania, too? New Caledonia goes with Australia. Everybody knows that."

"Well, then it obviously does *not* go with Asia, does it? Duh!"

"Oh, only an eight-year-old would say that." She pursed her lips. "Tell you what. Let's put New Guinea in Oceania. That means you get both Oceania and Australia. And I'll put in Egypt which gives me Africa."

"No way, Jose. Africa is worth more points than Australia and Oceania. And the game puts Egypt in the Middle East, not Africa."

"They speak African!"

"They speak Arabic!"

"Now I suppose you're going to say that because they speak English in the Philippines, that the Philippines go with Australia."

"The Philippines speak Tagalog, silly. Everybody knows that."

She put her hands on her hips. "Oh, you're so irascible."

"And you're an onanoko."

"You're mazhnun."

"Wa anti akthara miny."

"Sumashedshii malchik!"

"Mais plus d'intelligence que toi."

She caught her breath, and stamped a foot. "I'm telling Mom you said that!"

A grown-up thrust her head into the room. She barked without smiling. "Children, message from your mother on the recorder. You can listen to it in the office. And after you're done, gather your things. We are all getting in the van parked in front and leaving town due to the storm." As if in emphasis, a gust of wind shook the walls and the lights flickered.

Cheyenne and Burke looked out the window. Sheets of rain pelted the street between two large buildings.

In the office, Cheyenne pressed the Play button and listened. "You heard that?"

"Yeah. What's 'the tunnel system'?"

"I don't know. But it's underground."

"Most tunnels are. Duh." Burke frowned. "What should we do?"

"About what?"

"Mom is coming to pick us up. But Miss Mary just told us to get in the van. She's going to take us away."

Cheyenne thought. "I know. Let's get our stuff together, and then, if Mom still hasn't come, we'll ask Miss Mary to wait a while longer."

"What if Mom doesn't come?"

"Then maybe Carl will."

"He only did that once. And he was late. And he's not our Dad anyway. That's what he said."

"Mom will be here. Let's get our stuff."

When they were done, Burke said "My Silly Song collection. I can't leave it behind." Without waiting, he dove into the daycare's rumpus room.

Cheyenne followed. "Five minutes, Burke. And we need clothes and food, not books and toys."

Twenty minutes later they emerged with a Silly Song collection, a plastic plesiosaur, Six Stories by Dr. Seuss, a wooden Tic Tac Toe board, and Mr. Robocopter.

Opening the front door, they stepped onto the wind-swept porch of Miss Mary's Daycare.

The van was gone.

For a minute they stared. "Okay. How about this? There's a map in Miss Mary's office. Let's find the tunnel and go find Mom."

Burke brightened. "Moloditza. That's swell."

Cheyenne stepped back into the building and retrieved a thick plastic bag with drawstring. Placing their stuff inside, she removed her already rain-soaked summer dress and slipped on her emergency street clothes, to match Burke.

Within a few minutes they found a map of the city's downtown area, and within it, several yellow icons that read 'Tunnel Shelter.' One was located beneath the building just across the street.

Tossing their clothes and two Honey Buns into the sack with the other essentials, they braved the dark gusts and crossed. Inside the nave of the building they paused before an escalator whose downward movement had stopped. The lower end was steeped in darkness; a sound of flowing water emanated from its depths.

"Are you sure this is a good idea?"

Cheyenne took a deep breath. "You do have the lucky charm, don't you?"

Burke took it out of his pocket. He nodded.

Together they descended.

"Genechip?" asked Cliff. "As in 'Primal Lab genechip sitting in MacDonald Institute's basement Lab genechip'?"

Carm nodded, her back to the closed gateseal. "Yeah.

To the 'T'."

"But how the hell could that be?"

"Right on," said Bill. "What you showed us was a mosquito." He looked through the glass window. "That's one hell of a bite for a dang mosquito."

"They're fish. The next stage in Primal Lab's schedule. Last year we moved from bacteria to insects. Mosquitos were only the first of several aquatic insects that we were going to produce. We won't be finished with our work on insects for another year. The next stage was vertebrates, and they had to be aquatic, so that meant fish. Piranhas were on the list. But so were goldfish and guppies. How did we end up with these?"

"You're asking me?" said Cliff. "It's your project."

"Was. Miss Alice has been calling the shots ever since she got 'Nicky's' ear. Or some part of his anatomy."

"Didn't you say that it takes time to produce one of these monsters?"

She nodded.

"Who had time for that if the Array was working on insects?"

Carm looked slowly up. "That must be it. Someone in the Lab spent a lot of computer time processing the Life game to produce an algorithm that would manufacture piranhas."

"How's that again?"

"Ruben complained about the malfunctioning security system, the extended quarantines."

"So?"

"Don't your remember? That's the reason we're down here. Because of the twenty-four hour quarantine. That must be the answer. For months now, someone must have been inserting the experimental piranha genechip and running it for huge lengths of time, without Ruben or I knowing. That's what triggered the quarantines. Ruben thought it was a malfunction and blamed Bill. But there was no malfunction. The computer was merely doing what it was programmed to do, locking the doors for twenty-four hours each time someone secretly inserted the piranha genechip to steal computer time on the Array, probably every night for months."

"And the lights?"

"Like Bill said. Faulty transformer."

"But why?" asked Cliff. "Why would someone want to do that?"

"There's only one Array in existence. Plus only this computer has learned how to use the Life game to produce actual living creatures. Computers have to learn too, you know. That takes time."

"Then someone must have prepared the piranha genechip ahead of time, and put it back in the box of genechips scheduled for next year. And then...."

They looked at each other.

"Released them on us."

"Alice." Carm looked down.

"Not necessarily," said Cliff. "It could have been anyone at the Institute. Even MacDonald."

Ed slowly shook his head. His owl eyes stared. "It wasn't any person who did this. And it's not the computer. Oh, it was someone's hand that put in the piranha genechip. And it was a person who opened the gate to the tunnel to release the fish. But it was not their mind that was responsible." He looked around. "Can't you tell? Doesn't your soul sense the truth, and recoil from it? It's this place. This tunnel, which is like deep dark places everywhere. It's the spirits that inhabit such places and trick people into entering and losing themselves.

"Look." They stared as Ed continued. "The walls are flat and gray. They glide endlessly in the darkness turning, twisting, pressing in, waiting for lost souls to catch them in its traps, to suck them down into its watery depths and devour them. This is not the water we know; it's the water of death, of chaos. It comes from the other world, the spirit world, to surround us, and take us back with it. Those fish take not just our flesh, but our souls."

Marlena, who was staring into space, suddenly spoke. "Except the most innocent, those with the power to charm the spirits. Their touch can save souls."

The others stared into the rippling water that surrounded them. A row of narrow corridors stretched into the distance seeming to sink into the earth. Damp lights flickered and sparked in the gloom. Somewhere submerged bodies drifted, staring blankly at walls, their faces frozen in terror before unyielding gates.

"Whew," said Cliff, shaking the chills out of his back-bone, "I'm with Cracker on this. Do you think you can shut the fuck up?"

"Right on, dudes. We've got to go." Bill looked to the left and right. "Where's Mel?"

Gone.

Leaning inside each doorway they yelled. "Melanie!"

No one answered.

"All right. Which path do we take this time?"

A creak behind them made them turn.

"Look!" Carm pointed up and they saw the pull-chain slowly descend unaided.

"What the hell?"

"See? I told you. It's this place. It wants us."

"No. Look at that," said Carm, She pointed to an elec-tric diode that lit up just above the chain. "It's a central control switch. Someone somewhere is releasing the gateseal."

"Can they do that?"

"You want to wait to find out?"

"Let's move again, people. We don't want to be stand-ing here when that gate pops open."

"Ditto."

"Likewise."

As one, Carm, Bill, Cliff, Ed, and Marlena bolted down one of the corridors, thankful that the water was less deep than the section they had just traversed, but knowing that it was about to become deeper.

A minute passed and the corridor ended. They jerked to a stop.

"Well, if that don't beat everything–"

"Looks like we'll be able to order that taco after all."

Before them lay a fan-shaped pedestrian pavilion that accessed a ring of retail establishments. They had emerged at the outer edge of the curve, which extended several hundred feet before them to a relatively narrow aperture and a raised and open interior bathed in light. An assortment of tables and chairs occupied the pavilion, which was better lit than the corridors, but did not compare to the main area of the mall, which lay beyond. The sound of a musical band drifted from the main area through the aperture and across the intervening lake.

Behind them a metallic pop sounded within the corridor, and they knew the gateseal had opened. In another moment the water around their feet would be swarming with piranhas.

"Now what? We'll never make it across this stretch before those things arrive. The water is two feet deep."

"That's not enough for swimming."

"And it's too deep for running."

"Who can swim faster than piranhas anyway?"

Cliff looked at Bill. "I don't need to swim faster than them, dude, just faster than you."

Bill trembled. "No time for jokes, man. What do we do?"

Carm eyed the storefronts that curved away to right

and left. On one side her eye inspected each in turn: cell phones, bagels, coffee, stationery, printing. Down the other was men's clothing, jewelry, DVDs, books.

A sound like the susurrus of wind-swept leaves emanated from the corridor. It coalesced into a rough scraping of locusts. Carm chilled. For the fish to make such a sound, they must number in the thousands.

They sloshed to the left. The phone store seemed as good a refuge as any. Water filled the sales area, but surprisingly had failed to reach any of the cell phones that sat on display cases, several with screensavers working away as if it were an ordinary day. Carm and Cliff scrambled on top a large display case, while Bill went for the phones near the door.

"Maybe one still works," he yelled. He dialed 911. "Hey, it's ringing!"

"Great!"

"Yeah. Now we can get some help and get the heck out of this mess."

A tinny female voice answered. "Yes?"

"Hello! Is anyone there?"

"Who is this, please?"

"This is Bill. Wild Bill. I'm down here–" static drowned him out "–we're down here under the ground and there's a bunch of goldang fish all around us and we can't get out."

"Could you repeat your name, please? You're not coming through."

"I told you, it's Wild–" more static "–Bill. Ma'am, you've got to come get us out of here. We're in the tunnel system."

"Sir, the tunnels are closed for the night due to the hurricane." –static– "No one can get in or out. Now what's your problem?"

"It's the fish. The piranhas–"

"Fish? Fish need water, sir. There is no water in the tunnels because the tunnels are sealed."

"They're piranhas. And there is water–"

"Okay, kid. There are penalties for crank calls. I'm writing up a report. Your parents are gonna be fined by the city, and if you–" static again "–criminal charges. Good night, sir."

Bill put the phone down. "They hung up."

"Try again. We gotta make them understand."

Picking up the phone again, he redialed, then lowered the earpiece. "Static."

A nervous shriek came from the pavilion. Looking outside, they found that Marlena had climbed onto one of the pavilion tables and stood clear of the water. She held out her hands toward Ed. Ed stood between the table and the cell phone store. As they watched, the water changed color. From unlit but clear it suddenly shimmered with silver, as if the crescent of the pavilion had become the surface of the moon. Unlike the moon, however, the patches of silver drifted about, searching, listening. They encircled Ed.

"Ed!" yelled Carm. "Don't Move! They can't see you if you don't move, and they can't smell you if you have no open cuts."

Bill looked out and dropped the phone. "Dang," he said. "Dang!"

Ed froze. He held his breath. A swarm of piranhas carved a circle about his legs, eyeing him with curiosity. More collected. Several contacted his trousers, nibbled. Ed closed his eyes. Reaching into a pocket he slowly withdrew an intricately carved cross with a bundle of thread wound around the intersect and the upper limb to resemble an Egyptian ankh. He began to mutter spells and incantations while touching the talisman in various places.

Looking back at Carm, Bill yelled out, "We can't let this happen, Carm! We've got to *do* something."

"What, man? What *can* we do?" asked Cliff.

Bill snapped a finger. "They want blood? Maybe we can give em blood."

"What do you mean?"

Sliding down from the desk where he had taken refuge, Bill turned to a stack of cabinets. "I need a crowbar."

They looked around, shook their heads.

"Damn." He spotted something. "Wait just a dang minute." Moving carefully so as not to disturb the water and attract the fish into the store, Bill maneuvered behind a counter and took hold of a long metal bar intended for light fixtures. He moved back again. Placing one end behind the cabinets, he slowly pried them free.

"Look out. They're gonna hear this." With a wrench it broke free and slapped the water. The cabinet began to float.

With a rush some of the fish abandoned Ed.

Bill pushed the cabinet toward the door.

"It won't fit," called Carm. "The front doors–that cabinet. Too large."

Bill moved back to the desk, pressed a button and with a jerk the doors opened further. "Now all I need is a paddle and I'll be ready for the Rio Grande."

Carm and Cliff put one leg in the water, preparing to join.

"Keep your seats! This thing can only handle one hombre at a time. I'm gonna create a goldang diversion."

"No, Bill," said Carm. Cliff put a hand on her arm and she fell quiet.

Thrusting his makeshift raft through the doors, Bill poled to the coffeehouse. Once inside, he drifted to the kitchen. Arriving at the meat lockers, he yanked them open and inspected the contents. He yelled in triumph.

"Found it!"

The others waved, unable to see what he was up to.

Bill muttered. Removing several cases of half-thawed slabs of raw tuna, he tossed them into the water. Within a few minutes, the water was churning.

From atop the table, Marlena yelled. "It's working! There are much fewer here now." She looked sad again. "But still so many."

Within the coffee shop, Bill took up the metal pole again and climbed back on board the raft. He winced.

"What was that, Bill? Are you okay?"

"I'm fine, podners. Don't worry your mind." Bill poled back outside the shop, but the water around the raft now churned as violently as within. Spume splashed in Bill's face and he paused to wipe it off. He dropped the pole and it went under.

"Uh-oh. Now there's a problemo."

Marlena called out. "Ed, look! The piranhas are following Bill." Ed opened his eyes. Almost all the fish had left him. He ceased muttering.

"Over here. Quietly, but quickly. Get on the table with me. It's safe here." Putting his talisman back in his pocket, Ed climbed on the table with Marlena.

"Bill, wait! We'll come to you." Taking a cue from Bill, Carm and Cliff slid off the terraced display case where they had been sitting. Carm slid into the water and moved cautiously behind where she inserted another metal bar between the case and the floor. Cliff joined her and pulled. The case shook. The cell phones moved in their displays, spilling dust.

The case began to lean. Carm inserted and pulled again. Cliff pushed, and the case broke loose. Carm paused to rub dust from her eyes.

"Whoa!" Attempting to halt its collapse, Cliff reversed himself and pulled, but the heavy case yawed. He turned white. "Carm! Look out!" She glanced up to glimpse a wall of pine and mahogany expand to encompass her gaze. Pain shot through her skull as blackness came.

95

Chapter 9

At the bottom of the escalator, Cheyenne and Burke paused. The darkness was pervasive, only a single lonely fluorescent lamp set in the ceiling some hundred feet away cast its light upon the corridor. The passage was wide, at least twenty feet. Flanking the escalator, the tunnel continued in a line in either direction.

"I don't like this water, Cheyenne. There's something wrong with it."

"Well, Mom is down here somewhere and we have to find her."

Flowing out of the darkness, the water flowed like a tepid stream away from them, presenting its facade briefly to the dull flickering light before returning to more darkness.

"It isn't deep. I can see the bottom."

"But how far must we walk? And what if it gets deeper? I don't swim so good."

Cheyenne leaned over the side of the escalator. Her eye roamed over the scene. The far wall of the corridor was blank, offering no relief. Several shops interrupted the near wall.

"Look, Burke!" Peering to one side they saw through glass doors a collection of sports equipment. The interior was dark. "Maybe we can find something to help us." Reluctantly, they entered the water and slogged to the glass doors. The flow of the water had pried them from their runners and one had vanished, presumably now lying flat beneath the water.

"It's so dark, Cheyenne. I can't see anything in here."

"Wait a minute." She approached a light switch.

"You're not going to touch that with your hand, are you, silly?"

She paused. "Oh, yeah." She laughed. They stood on a dry countertop. Reaching for a plastic bat, she flicked the switch. The lights burst on, casting a bright glow throughout the store.

"Wonderful!" they clapped.

Burke moved one leg toward the water.

"You're not going to put your leg in the water, are you silly?"

"Oh, yeah," he laughed. Slowly they each inserted a finger, then their arms. "It's okay. The wiring must be in the ceiling."

They walked around. "We need a flashlight." At length they had to acknowledge that they could find none.

"What's next? Do we start walking?"

"In case you haven't noticed, Einstein, the water level is rising. Since we can't find a flashlight, I think a boat would be a better idea."

"Swell! We'll float just like the discoverers of Micronesia, navigating by the stars."

"There are no stars, here, silly Burke." She looked back out at the corridor. "This isn't that kind of night. But a different kind."

Another search of the contents of the shop ensued.

"Il n'y a pas de boat aussi."

"Oui. Une catastrophe. And my feet are getting cold."

Cheyenne put one hand to her chin. She looked around till her eyes came to a wire stand filled with volleyballs. It slowly drifted. Several of the balls had tumbled out and now littered the store.

"Quelle fortune!" Approaching, she began to remove the balls. "These float well and will support us, but how will we hold them together?"

"The wire cage." Burke unfolded the cage. Placing all the balls they could find onto the wire, they then folded the other half of the cage across the top to imprison them.

Cheyenne frowned. "We can't sit on bare wire. And what's to hold it together?"

Burke sighted a square section of wooden flooring that had come loose. "There." They maneuvered it on top of the caged volleyballs.

Cheyenne held up her hands. "And rope to hold it all together." Cheyenne and Burke quickly tied the whole, bending the wires where necessary to keep the balls from slipping out.

"Voila. U nas yest boat."

"You're still mazhnun—crazy. But it's time to go." Depositing their sack of supplies on the wooden plank, they selected two badminton rackets encased in covers to serve as paddles. Grabbing a few extra items, they pushed the raft into the corridor, and leaped on.

They began to move. In another moment they were drifting with the current, away from the comfort of the lights, and into shadow. For a brief minute the overhead fluorescents sparked and flickered, offering a last glimpse of the world they knew. The corridor turned and a new world took shape.

"Cheyenne. I'm afraid."

"Silly, Burke. There's nothing...to be...afraid of." Her voice trembled. Blackness enveloped them, and for a time there was nothing but the sound of water trickling from the ceiling, and obscure creaking, and the current flowing around nameless obstacles. A gray wall emerged from nowhere and they bumped into it. Hardly pausing, the current carried them off again.

An overhead flashed once to reveal a flooded corridor strewn with stray debris and a maze of intersecting walkways. Then it died and the blackness returned. The raft bumped, turned, rebounded.

"How can we find anyone down here?"

"Faith, Burke. She's here. I can feel it."

"Yes? But there's more. I feel something else." Burke pulled out the lucky charm and together they clasped it.

The raft drifted into a wider space where the overheads glowed steadily but were so dim as to be almost useless. They stopped drifting.

"What happened? Cheyenne, we're not moving. And it has gotten so cold."

"I don't know. But don't put your hand in the water. I think we should sit still and keep quiet."

Slowly the walls receded. Forms coalesced, outlines emerged. Suddenly a familiar figure stood before them. It held out its hand. "So there you are, Cheyenne and Burke. I've been looking all over for you. Such naughty children you are to lead your Miss Mary on a wild search." Miss Mary stood before them in every detail. She held out a comforting hand. "Now take my hand. It's time for us to go. Your parents will be very upset for your disappearing like you did."

Burke's hand began to rise. Cheyenne struck it down. "You're not Miss Mary."

Mary looked at them quizzically. "Of course I am, silly Cheyenne. Who else would I be?"

"Miss Mary left in a van. She took the other kids and left town. They left to get away from the storm."

"Oh? And are you sure they didn't leave to get away from *you*?"

"She left because of the hurricane. She forgot us."

Mary stopped smiling. She stepped forward, more insistent. "Give me your hand. Now."

Cheyenne lifted a racket. "It isn't you. You can't be down here. Stay away."

Miss Mary dropped her hand. She melted into shadow.

Burke and Cheyenne took up the rackets and hesitantly dipped them into the water. They stroked, but the raft only revolved in a circle. The walls coalesced again.

A voice came from behind. "Why I don't believe this, what are you kids doing down here? Don't you know this place isn't safe?"

They turned.

Carl stood before them. "Well, am I glad I found you. That's enough of this nonsense. It's time to give me your hands so I can take you away, to someplace much better."

Open-mouthed, they made no move.

"With ice cream. And cake." Carl smiled his best pretty boy smile. "And balloons." He reached behind his back and produced two bright red balloons.

They closed their mouths and pulled back. "No."

Carl hesitated. Smiling grander than ever, he took a step toward them. "But isn't this what you want? To come with me to visit places and get lots of treats. I can show you lots of places, strange places, where things happen that you've never dreamed of." Carl stopped smiling. "Isn't that what you've always wanted since your dad died? A new dad who will be there always and forever, a real dad all to yourself. Me?"

Cheyenne shook back the tears. "Carl's not our dad. He didn't pick us up. And he wouldn't be down here helping us." She looked at Carl's feet, which rested on the water without breaking its surface. "And you–you're not even Carl."

Carl frowned. "Then who would I be, little ones?"

"I don't know. But we're not coming with you. Stay away."

Carl melted into blackness.

Several minutes passed. The walls returned and the raft began to move. Drifting out of the room, it entered another unlit corridor that seemed to flow on forever.

Something cracked.

"What was that?" Cheyenne's voice trembled even more. Burke's face appeared, framed by the glow of fluorescent automobile nightsticks. "Oh, so that's how they work."

Burke pulled the wooden Tic Tac Toe board out of the sack and they selected their pieces and played to the glow of the nightsticks, the lucky charm between them. They began to sing as they floated. "This old man, he played one, he played knick-knack on my thumb. With a knick-knack paddywack, give the dog a bone, this old man came rolling home..."

Carl backed away from the gateseal, shaking. He glanced down at his pocket where the gun rested. The pedestrians, still tending to those injured by the bikers, were too distracted by the chaos to notice him. The plan that had occurred to him while in Ray's pickup returned to mind. He made for the Emporia Bank lobby.

The lobby was deserted. Outside, a dark tide pressed in on the glass walls and the lights flickered as water penetrated power lines. Debris flew past with increasing force.

He zipped his jacket and plunged into the morass.

Piecing his way along a raised wall that paralleled the sidewalk, he soon arrived at his destination. He entered the building and climbed deserted stairs to the second floor. He found the office he sought. The stenciling read 'Tunnel Console.' In smaller letters beneath, 'Pass Required.' He smiled and knocked on the glass.

In answer, a police officer folded a newspaper and rolled his chair to the microphone. "Hey, Carl. What's happenin'? Haven't seen you in a while, pal."

Carl waved at him through the security glass. Mouthed some words. The dull roar of the storm was sufficiently loud that he could have been drowned out. The officer pressed a button allowing him entry.

"Hi, Brad! Yes, it *has* been a while." Carl grinned. They shook hands and Carl sat. "Well, what do you think? Will there be anything left of the city after all this?"

"We'll find out in the morning. What brings you here on a night like this?"

"Oh, I just ran into Captain Olsen and he suggested that I come down here and get deputized and see if I could help out. He said the department's short-handed, and he's worried since every assignment is understaffed tonight. Although I'm not sure what I can do...maybe start by grabbing you some coffee?"

"He said that? That's sorta against procedure, Carl. I'm gonna have to check this out."

Carl shrugged. Casually, he looked past Brad at the panel of the video screens. "What are these here?"

Brad paused, hand on phone. "Locking switches. Switch one of them suckers and you seal off a section of the tunnel. Or rather one door—gateseals we call 'em. It takes at least two switches to seal off a section."

"Have you closed any sections yet?"

He nodded. "Most of 'em are already closed. Tonight's the night. We got a few calls earlier from sections where the videos are down complaining that a little water has gotten in. So we shut those down some time ago. All that's left is the Mall and the Emporia and a few surrounding sections."

"Don't say."

"Yeah. It's better to be safe than sorry. The Mayor and police chief want everything sealed up before things get outta hand, like what happened last year. The chamber of commerce screams bloody murder when they get a little rain on their parade. Heh! I expect this time I'll get a medal for keeping the tunnel dry. And that's good, cause the Mayor himself is down there with a bunch of commissioners just to prove the shelters are safe."

"What's that big button there?"

"Drainage. Opens onto the county spillway. Of course, right now the spillway is higher than street level. If you were to punch that one, there'd be a whole lot of nothing below. Davy Jones all the way. No more commissioners–and no more Mayor!"

"And those?"

"Emergency releases. To interrupt the automatic locking mechanisms. This here is the master switch, under the plastic case."

Brad put the phone to his ear. "Anyway, I gotta check you out, Carl. You understand."

Carl gripped Brad's arm. "Look at your console, Brad. Isn't that the tunnel beneath the Emporia Bank?"

Brad put on spectacles and peered. The remains of Dicker's bike still sputtered flames. Brad caught his breath. "Son of a bitch! I gotta report this!" The lights flickered again and he put the phone to his ear. "Dammit! The phones are out. Watch things for me, Carl." He leaped to his feet and rushed out.

Carl eyed the corners of the ceiling.

No videocams.

Scooting his chair forward, he examined each screen in turn. Several showed people milling about in the well-lit sections of the tunnel. Others showed poorly lit areas. About half the screens were black, entirely without power. His eye paused on the panels showing the sections beneath the Emporia. In one screen laymen tended to several injured people lying next to an escalator—the Emporia. In another, the flaming wreck threw smoke into the adjoining corridor. A third revealed a body lying prone before an exercise spa. Jimbo. Carl glanced at Brad's crumpled sports section. His brows arched.

While he watched, a series of yellow lights flicked on, and in the screens he noticed a half dozen gates begin to close. Words flashed on the LCD at eye level: 'Warning.

Water levels approaching maximum tolerance. Gateseals closing.'

Carl reached up and popped the protective cover off the emergency release master switch. He snapped it. The flashing LCD changed to red: 'Warning. Gateseal closure interrupted. Water levels exceeding maximum.'

Pulling more switches, he inspected the Emporia to verify that only the several sections of tunnel around the Emporia remained sealed. One by one, the other screens began to wink out as various sections of the tunnel filled with water.

Next Carl glimpsed what he had hoped to see: two Harleys motoring through a section of tunnel–Cole's bike, and the bike Carl had abandoned. They were headed away from the Emporia, toward its sister bank, the Imperial. Carl flicked a switch and the gateseal to the Imperial began to swing shut. The bikes braked, reversed. Taking another turn, they accelerated. Carl snickered. He flicked another switch and sealed that escape route as well. He could almost hear their yells of frustration as Ray, Cole, Leroy and Griff shook little black and white fists at the videocams. How he wished he had an intercom!

Carl let his hand wander across the console and it came to rest on the Drainage button. For a moment he reflected on the weightiness of the deed. Many of the sections contained people of all ages. And apparently much of the city's elite, though not visible from the Console. Then he glanced at the biker gang, speeding to imagined safety.

He pressed it.

Immediately, the upper left-most screen displayed a huge wall of water crashing through an interior space, and the screen winked out. Another followed; then another. From chamber to chamber, corridor to corridor, the wall of water crashed. The basement of the Emporia was soon swamped. Within minutes it covered the escalator where the injured lay, churning pedestrians and the injured about like chaff.

Turning to the gateseal at the Imperial–the one he had just closed to stop Ray–Carl released the lock to reopen it. The wall of water from the Drainage area crashed through the corridor with irresistible force. On the screen he could see Ray look back in terror, the bikers accelerating to escape. Leroy tossed Griff over to lighten the load—the flood consumed him.

With glee, Carl slammed another gate shut and watched as the bikes skidded to a halt to wait in despair as their doom approached. It slammed into them with the force of a jackhammer, tossing their bodies about like dolls. In the screen he watched Ray struggle underwater, his fists losing strength, his eyes glazing over. The screen went black, and Carl chuckled. Finally he released the gateseal.

Damn, that felt good.

Carl noted with satisfaction that one section in the tunnel remained sealed and dry–'Sweats-R-Us'.

Footsteps sounded. Carl steeled himself and slid behind the office door.

"Carl? Huh. Wonder where he went." Brad crossed to the console and leaned over, adjusting his glasses. He stiffened. "What the goddamhell?!"

Deftly, Carl placed his gun to Brad's head, and fired. The policeman collapsed over a gory console. Carl slipped quietly away.

Chapter 10

The darkness flashed and Carm stretched one hand to flick on her computer screen and see her voicemail. Dank water streamed from her outstretched arm and she started. Losing her grip on boards that barely held together, she went under, in another moment re-emerging to gasp and clamber on again.

Then she remembered. Surrounding her were gray walls that stretched and multiplied without end; below her lurked cold liquid that descended into blackness. How could the water be so deep? It should be no more than a few feet, enabling her to stand if she wished. The tunnel itself could be no more than ten feet high, most of which arched overhead. But her feet had not contacted any floor. Or had they?

She wiped grime and liquid away from her eyes and a large knot that had risen on her temple. Like her marriage, she was no longer sure of anything. In the darkness, faces appeared in the flash of transformers to mock her, only to fade and recede into nothing. She grimaced. Ed was too modest; he had not been wrong. If only she had listened...

Exhaustion crept upon her. Alongside, a silver blur took shape, staring with its lifeless eyes, before drifting away. Let them come, Carm thought. She could not prevent her limbs trailing in the water in any event and after so many hours of desperate flight she had no more will or energy to continue. *Come get me,* she thought. *I will no longer resist.*

But the piranhas did not, but passed by in their hundreds, and, adrift on her boards, she was dimly aware that the current was taking her through a labyrinth of flooded passageways, and apparently away from her companions since she could hear no trace of them, and away from the sweet siren call that she had heard when in the mall, the source of the music and a promise of safety.

A wall loomed. The boards bumped it and shuddered, but held. Spinning about like in an amusement ride, she grew dizzy, then the current took her again and she plunged back into the labyrinth. The lights died and she floated in blackness, nothing to feed her senses but the coldness of the water. Could it be possible that she still lived?

Somewhere in the recesses of her mind she knew that no such place could exist beneath the city, that these could not be the tunnels she knew of, not the city tunnels that she and her companions had entered. Therefore, they must be something else. Which meant she was *somewhere* else. Where, she wondered, her eyes straining for a glimmer of light. What might the Pit hold for the unwary who wander into its realm?

For a time there was nothing but the sound of water trickling from the ceiling, and obscure creaking. Then the corridor widened and the current took her into the middle of a wide dark space whose walls receded into impenetrable blackness, a small dim circle of light doing nothing to relieve her sense of complete isolation, as exposed as a wound. The raft stopped moving.

Carm wiped her forehead and suppressed a rising sense of panic. She shifted her weight. She extended one foot to test the depths again, but something within her halted the effort and cautioned her not to move. This place was not safe. Her limbs grew colder, their numbness edging closer like something sensate, as if a contagion had seized her flesh. She focused so intently on the pain in her legs that a minute passed before she realized that a man stood before her and that he had been watching her from some moments.

The suit threw her off at first, but the shock of white hair, the withered skin, and the arrogant turn of lip were unmistakable.

Boss-Man.

"Mr. MacDonald!" she gasped. Her voice broke and she began to cry. At last she would get free, escape her tormentors, since Nicholas could not have walked far into the tunnels. Given his frailty, an exit must lie close, perhaps the very chamber that she had been about to enter when... But what had happened to her? And how had she become separated from her companions? She recalled nothing except that she had awakened on these boards floating in this Abyss.

"Miss Niles," he grinned. "I knew you would not let me down. Come now, we have an important engagement to attend. Some very important people are waiting for us and it won't do to make them wait." He extended his hand, waiting expectantly.

Carm smiled, but hesitated. The numbness increased and she wondered how Mr. MacDonald could be towering so far above the surface of water that a moment before had threatened to engulf her. "Yes. Mr. MacDonald, of course. I'll just..." She paused again, still confused. He was standing on the surface of the water. Defying the black liquid, his shoes were entirely dry. She shook her head to clear it. "Mr. MacDonald, where were you?"

A moment passed. "Where was I?"

"After the storm hit, you disappeared. Where did you go?"

His expression remained as constant as a star. "I attended a reception. I attended a reception. The Mayor was there."

"How did you get there, Mr. MacDonald? The building shut down when the storm hit, and the streets were flooded. How did you leave the Institute?"

MacDonald seemed suddenly paler, and his voice weakened. "I attended a reception. A gala reception." As Carm watched, he drifted backward into blackness and vanished.

The lights died and for a minute the makeshift raft rotated slowly, and Carm struggled to control her panic. Covering her face with her hands, she peeked through every few seconds for a return of the light, while her legs expected an imminent return of the pale jewels and their annihilating teeth. She thought of Ed and his warning of the Abyss and its waters of chaos and shivered. When the lights came on again, she opened her eyes, thankful for anything that would dispel the gloom.

A figure backed into her sight, his leather jacket gleaming like new, hair smoothed back as if ready to tackle the day. He turned. The boyish smile flashed far brighter than the overheads and reminded her of that day months before when he had first come to her, rescuing her from her dreams while she glowered in the park beside the Institute. Carl had seemed like a messenger from heaven on that overcast winter day. And might have remained so, had she not learned that duplicity was his nature and that she could not depend on him for the simplest task.

"Look at you, gal! You fill out a swimsuit like no one I've ever seen. What do you say we find a nice dry spot somewhere and fall in lust for a while?" He grinned his best smile and stepped closer. The water covered his shoes and he kicked up a ripple.

"Are you kidding?" She managed to frown and she shook her head. "I mean you're kidding, right?" Behind him was only blackness. "Where are the kids, Carl?"

He stopped smiling. "The kids? Your kids are fine, Carm. Your kids are fine."

"Where are they, Carl? You were supposed to get them. That's where I was going when I ended up down here...wherever here is."

"There was no need to get them, Carm. Cheyenne and Burke have been here, down here, waiting for you. I came down here to meet them and together we've been waiting. We knew you would come."

Carl raised one hand and a portion of the darkness behind him began to glow. Soon two small figures took shape. A pretty girl in a bright summer dress skipped forward. Behind scampered an impish shadow.

"Hi, Mommy," sparkled Cheyenne. "You've finally come."

Tears formed in Carm's eyes. "Hi, baby. Is it...is it really you?"

"Mommy, I don't like it when you talk like that," said Cheyenne. "You worry me."

The tears gushed.

"Me three," added Burke. Extracting a slingshot from his pocket he let fly a marble. A jet of light daggered above her to vanish in the depths of the limitless night. "I don't like you talking like this." He halted and stared, vulnerable. "Mommy...I want you. I want you to hold me."

"I want to hold you too, baby." Of their own accord, her arms lifted towards him.

"Did you like your ice cream, kids? And your red balloons?" Carl beamed down upon them with a grand smile.

"Yeah! You're the best dad any kid ever had! Can we go back to the toy store now and buy some more stuff?"

"You bet, little ones." Carl looked at Carm, a serious

look settling on him. "But only if Mommy joins us." He straightened. "Mommy has to join us."

The children looked at Carm. "Yes. Mommy has to join us."

Gushing tears, Carm raised her head. "Mommy cannot join you, babies, because you are not real. You are not Cheyenne and Burke. And you are not Carl. And Carl would not be here. And Carl would not be saying such things even if he were."

Cheyenne and Burke glided backward into the night to vanish.

Carl advanced another pace. "You're talking nonsense, dear Carm. If I am not Carl, who would I be? Don't I look like Carl? Don't I sound like Carl? Aren't I the image of what you want most in the world, an attractive man, a devoted husband, a good and kind father with time to spend with your kids? A man who won't die like your first husband did—when he *deserted* you?"

The darkness of her dreams returned in a savage rush and images of the funeral and her standing alone in the drizzle of autumn with two small children by a headstone flooded her mind with long-suppressed memories. The promise of the future that had died on that day! She had thought she had recovered, regained her balance, but the darkness of the night brought it back. Always back. And the rain. The night, and the rain, and deep dark places where she could not see the light.

"I have no husband. He died and is gone. There is only

Carl, but now I know that he too is an illusion, even in daylight. And you are not Carl. Or Cheyenne, or Burke."

The thing standing before her frowned. Its voice rose, "Then who would we be, Miss Niles?" In quick succession, a series of images flashed before her: MacDonald, Alice, Cheyenne, Carl, Ruben, Gary, Miss Mary, Burke, then Carl again.

She found she was screaming "Stop stop it!" with her hands over her ears, then the images vanished and the blackness returned. Calm returned and she was no longer afraid, even though she could see the silver blurs collecting again about the raft. They eyed her hungrily. "I don't know who you are," she said, "but you are no one I know, or care to meet. And you cannot keep me down here for I will swim. I will run, paddle, or crawl out of this place until I find my children and not you or anything will stop me."

As she flung her words into the darkness, she felt the coldness ease, and the darkness lift, and in another moment the current returned and she found her raft was wending strange pathways again.

"Carm!" shouted Cliff. Shoving with all his strength, he sought to lift the display case. "Ed, Marlena, I need help." He pushed again, without result. "I can't move it."

Marlena stood on the table with her hands over her mouth. Ed kissed his talisman, slipped back into the water and soon joined Cliff. Together they attempted to lift the case out of the water.

"It's no use. The water has added too much weight. Only a crane could lift it now." Cliff gave up.

"No, it's still attached to the wall." Ed pointed to twisted metal and inserted the bar again. Soon the case came loose with a snap.

They gazed blankly at the dark surface.

"Where is she?"

Ed shook his head.

"The water is only a couple feet deep."

"The lights are dim. She could have drifted into a corner."

Searching, they found nothing. Clambering onto the now floating display, they poled outside and joined Marlena. They shook their heads as Marlena jumped on. A hundred feet away Bill lay motionless upon his own makeshift raft.

"Hold on, Bill! We're coming!"

Their raft was clumsy and rotated to foil their efforts, but at last they arrived beside Bill. He lay on the cabinet and stared.

"What are you waiting for? Jump!"

"You may not want me to." Bill swung one leg free of the water where it had been dragging. The lower half was gone. "I cut myself in there. Didn't get free of the water in time."

"Oh, Wild Bill."

"I'm afraid now it's simply Bill."

"We'd better go now," said Cliff.

"We can't."

The others looked at Marlena. She was staring back at the cell phone store. "She is there."

"Carm?" said Cliff. "We looked. She's gone. Or drowned and underwater."

"You will find her now. If you look." Transferring Bill onto their larger raft, they poled back to the cell phone store.

"There!" shouted Bill, forgetting his own pain.

Peering through the gloom, they saw a dark shape float through the entrance.

"It's her!"

Quickly they dragged Carm on board, mindful of the liquid eyes that watched.

She suddenly coughed, vomiting water, and groaned. She sat up.

Marlena spoke. "We have to leave. This place..." She cast her glance all around. "None of this is safe any longer." They looked down and noticed that the water level was at least three feet and rising, and that the entire lake was infested with a growing crowd of darting silver jewels.

They began to pole across the remaining distance to the well-lit, beckoning aperture and its happy, happy music.

Arriving at the terminus of the dark waters, the threshold where the golden music emanated, Cliff, Ed, and Marlena slid off, avoiding any contact with the water and the sheening multitude filling its depths. Helping Carm, and carefully lifting Bill, they abandoned the display case. They placed Bill on the well-polished upraised floor of the mall. Carm looked at the scene in amazement.

On the platform, incomparably wide compared to the narrow interiors through which they had labored, mingled a throng of people attending the Mayor's Event in the city tunnel. Some wrung water out of jackets and sweaters, and a few looked as though they preferred to be elsewhere, but most stood and laughed or sat on the many dining chairs that dotted the platform, in no way worried by the hurricane.

An endless supply of treats was served by waiters and waitresses from a variety of fast-food restaurants that ringed them, and pizza trays and hot dog buns lay scattered like so many victims of some culinary battle. In the center, confirming their ears–if their eyes still refused to believe–sat a gaily dressed orchestra belting out popular tunes.

Beside them tuxedo-dressed dignitaries clustered around several spanking new all-terrain Land Rovers under bright display lights that entirely countered the hexwork of strong plastiglass panes that served as the mall's ceiling, and upon which Carm could see torrents of rain fall. Balloons popped in time with bottles of champagne.

"–pleased to announce the kicking off of my new campaign for mayor by making a donation of the proceeds from the sale of these two vehicles to my campaign fund. And I thank you, Mr Beckman, for your kind contribution. The automobile dealership business is one of the most important industries in our fair city–"

The band struck up another number while cameras flashed.

Carm took a few steps onto the platform and halted, stunned. The others collected behind her, Cliff and Ed tying cloth napkins around Bill's leg.

Cliff shook his head, "I don't know about you, but I don't want to stay here. The water is rising, Carm."

"You're more right than you know," said Carm. "They are hungry and they are coming. Someone has to warn them."

Ed looked at Marlena. She stood in a trance, looking towards the invisible world threatening to engulf them. "We're still not safe. This place is not safe. Only a few minutes remain." Suddenly, she turned and looked straight at the water about fifty feet distant. She paled. The others looked but saw nothing. A look of horror on her face, she resumed staring up and beyond.

Cliff approached several persons sitting around a table. "Sorry to disturb you folks, but we need help. Our friend's been hurt. He needs a doctor."

No one replied.

"Excuse me, but does anyone know if there's a doctor in here?"

They ignored him, continuing their muffled conversation.

"Look, I don't want to be rude, but we're in real trouble. Can you at least look at me!"

He retreated.

Cliff looked at Carm. "Wh...Why don't they answer? And why can't I hear them clearly? Their talk–it's dull and weak as if coming from a long way off. But I'm standing right next to them."

Marlena spoke. "Because they don't see you. Because we come from there." She pointed to the water. "From the spirit world. But they will see us."

She looked at Ed and he pulled the talisman from his pocket. He touched it in various places, and in another moment the conversations of everyone in their vicinity ceased. The crowd turned and looked at the newcomers. Several persons with EMS uniforms quickly appeared and came to Bill. Soon, however, the rest resumed their conversing and ignored them again, and the band resumed playing.

Carm sighted His Honor, The Mayor. "We have to talk to the Mayor. Only he can order these people out." With Cliff, Ed, and Marlena, she began to push her way through the crowd. The party-goers retreated before them, visibly disgusted.

"Oh, street-people. They'll live anywhere."

"There oughta be a law. Is there no place we can go without being harassed by these pan-handlers?"

"Why be politically correct, my dear? They're just

bums!"

The Mayor turned.

"Your Honor," said Carm. "I...um, my name's Carmen Niles. We–"

He signaled the band to stop. Smiling, he glanced quickly at her soiled attire. "Yes, my dear? Speak up. But please be brief, this is a *special* occasion." He glanced around, waved his hand to a photographer to indicate a pause in the picture-taking.

"We've been in the tunnel, sir. We barely made it through. The piranhas..."

A look of puzzlement took over. "The what?"

"Fish, sir. Piranhas. They're coming, they're in the water now, and the level's rising, and it's coming this way, and you've got to get these people out of here right now before it's too late!"

Cliff nodded. "It's all true, Your Honor. Our friend's been hurt."

His Honor's brows raised. "Oh, how dreadful. We have emergency personnel for this sort of thing. Have you told them?"

"Yes...but we're all in danger here!"

The Mayor hesitated. He glanced about. Several security police moved closer, sporting serious looks. "How's the water situation, gentlemen?"

"Under control, Mr. Mayor. All the sections were sealed two hours ago. Only a little water got in."

"Any other problems?"

"Just a few hooligans by the Emporia. It was reported an hour ago. We've heard nothing since."

He smiled. "There. You see, Miss Niles, you have nothing to worry about. The water is under control. We are perfectly safe."

"But the fish, sir! Piranhas are coming. They're already here." She pointed behind her to the darkened aperture leading to the bowels of the tunnel system. The raft had drifted away and was no longer visible. "They're there, right there, in the water. We can stand here debating, sir, but in a few minutes they'll be here! Among us! You've got to evacuate everyone now!"

The Mayor stopped smiling. "Now, look. I understand that your friend has been hurt. But I'm in no mood for gags."

"It's not a gag, sir," said Ed. "It's piranhas, all right. They've come to take us to the spirit world. Marlena is having a vision of them right now." Marlena stared into the distance.

"'Piranhas'?"

They nodded.

"Back there, you say?" The Mayor nodded toward the darkness.

"Yes, sir. They're right behind us."

Ed nodded. "I have my talisman, but it can't protect us much longer."

The Mayor and his friends looked at each other silently. The smile returned. "My dear Miss Niles, it was good of you to take the time to warn us of these... 'piranhas'. I will take it under advisement. Now, maybe you should see to your ill friend and make sure he's taken care of. Have some refreshment. The bagels are the best anywhere!"

The matter was disposed of. The suits walked away, leaving Carm and the others alone.

Chapter 11

Melanie ran. Without pause or thought, her legs pumped, lifting, leaping, splashing, to carry her through to other, safer regions where no jewels with eyes or knives lay in wait. Her lungs heaved, reassuring her that her perfect limbs were intact, unmarred by the bright clinging ornaments that had confused the others.

But there were no others. None could have survived.

Melanie ran. Never had she known such terror. Not in her worst nightmares of waiting for Terry to pick her up in strip club parking lots at three in the morning, not in the knife fights where the bloodied loser shot up the joint and hunted grimly for survivors, not in the deep dark memories of her father playing the secret games that no one was supposed to know and that hurt so much and who appeared like a ghost in the eyes of every stranger.

Stumbling around a corner, she paused, her lungs and her legs finally giving out. Her eyes spun, hoping for some relief from the numbing gray walls that stubbornly refused to end. Above her head flashed broken lamps to reveal an endless corridor that stretched from darkness to shadow, strewn with nameless debris floating eternally on its sluggish midnight surface. Across her feet flowed dark cold water.

For a time she staggered aimlessly. Then her eyes fell on a series of doors. Inside was a dark mysterious chamber, with shiny surfaces that occasionally flashed so bright that they blinded her, always to die and fade back into murky depths. From somewhere a dull glow shined, and she detected row upon serried row of dials and knobs, among them instruments of death, neatly ordered as by some evil intelligence, and she squeezed herself into a corner, seeking to disappear into the waist-deep water.

Only her eyes remained clear. So she could see the lurkers before they struck. Spy them in their lairs to swim past and escape. She closed her eyes. Shuddered. How long had they lurked? How long had they watched and spied? She sank deeper into the corner until only her pupils were exposed, chameleon eyes that watched above and below.

From far away an alien whispering grew. She trembled. The jewels would find her if she remained, consume her perfect flesh. She spotted a patch of blackness, and crept within. Finding a handle, she slowly, quietly, closed it.

"Found it!" said the alien, slyly muffling its voice. "This tuna is half thawed. But it'll do the goldang job."

Other aliens shouted faint gibberish from a distance.

The first alien clattered around with its knife, trolling the water to catch her. She closed her eyes tight.

"Ouch!...I'm fine, podners. Don't worry your mind."

The alien gave up and left.

At length all noise stopped and the water grew calm and she felt she could risk lifting the handle. The strain she had placed on her body in the enclosure was telling, and her limbs, her fair lovely limbs that evoked such admiration that fools in their Sunday best would stuff the last of their minimum wage dollars into her panties, even her limbs said it was time to move, to take a chance lest the enclosure twist and break them.

She touched the handle. With a start it sprang open—but she remained imprisoned. Through a metal grill she peered from an impossibly small refuge, staring up from its tiny cage like a predator's next meal. And saw him. Her husband, Terry, impromptu metal crutch propping him up, shards glinting in his arm, lurched out of the darkness, framed by endless gray walls, and glared at her with her father's ghost eyes.

Staggering forward, he thumped the crutch like an angry club. One hand grabbed the cupboard and lifted both her and her prison with impossible strength. For a moment Mel stared suspended in air at what was left of Terry after the silver jewels had finished. The flesh was horribly mangled but somehow the eyes still stared and the jaws still worked.

"You left me, Mel. You stuffed their money in your crotch, and you left me." The ghost eyes glanced down where the dark sluggish water swarmed with a cloud of bright gnashing teeth. Slowly, he lowered the cage. A muffled scream escaped through its bars as the jewels rushed in.

FRENZY

Casting a last glance about to ensure he was not observed, Carl inserted the crow bar between the two plates and pried. The air conditioning vent split apart. Climbing inside, he clung to the edge, then allowed himself to slide. In a few moments, he stopped sliding. Checking his flashlight, he again took up the bar and placed his feet against a grille. With a grunt, he popped it out. He let his legs dangle, and dropped.

The lights on Sweats-R-Us were on half power, but more surprising was the lack of water on the floor, which remained dry. He smiled. The gateseals worked. Slowly and with elaborate casualness in case others had found a refuge among the bicycles and exercise paraphernalia, he stalked to the locker room.

Locker two twenty-one stood open.

Carl smiled. Producing the crow bar, he placed it inside the lock of locker two twenty-two. It clanged open and he breathed deep. Inside was an exercise bag, and Carl lifted it out, noting the weight indicative of something besides clothing. He unzipped it.

Inside was a large stack of $100 bills with 'Xmas' scribbled across, and a smaller stack of $100 bills with the word 'party.' A shoebox lay beside. Opening the shoebox, he peered at a white powder that had been carefully sealed in several layers of plastic. He smiled again.

This bitch is mine.

Replacing the top to the shoebox, Carl put all the items, including Jimbo's gun, inside the bag and zipped it.

FRENZY

He returned to the exercise room, approached the air conditioning shaft, and paused. The shaft was fifteen feet high. Even if he could gain it, there was no way he could slide back up. He frowned. He had not thought this far ahead. For a moment he chilled as he recalled the irresistible wave of water that had drowned Ray and the others, which he had unleashed. But, he reassured himself, the gateseals for this section were closed. The lack of water on the floor of Sweats-R-Us was testament to that.

Still, it would not do to be in the vicinity when morning came, and the water drained away, as it surely would, and the gateseals eventually opened. It was best to skip town now. It would be days before he was missed, and he might even be presumed dead.

A new life awaited.

But how to grasp it? Nervously, he entered the corridor, carefully shielding his face from the videocams. At the far end, where Dicker's body still lay, the gateseal creaked from the enormous pressure of the spillway. Carl chilled again.

Re-entering the exercise room, he paused. A small bell had sounded with a ring that was eerily familiar. Venturing into a back supply room, he was surprised to see an elevator. All the times that he had come here, he thought, he had never entered this room, never suspected it existed. Well, one cannot argue with good timing. Stepping to the door, he pressed the button.

The carriage arrived, and he entered.

Inside, beside the door, were two buttons: '1' and 'T'. Being already in the tunnel, he punched '1'. Slowly the doors shut until the dim light seeping in from the exercise place was extinguished, relieved only by an even dimmer light from interior flourescents. The carriage lurched and Carl stepped back, jealously cradling his package.

He frowned. He was not headed up, but down. He punched '1' again. Then 'T'. Then both repeatedly. The carriage kept dropping, not accelerating, but slowly, steadily, and the bell rang once, then twice, then several more times till Carl lost count and put his palms to his head to block out the sound.

Finally, the bell ceased and the carriage came to a stop. Angrily, Carl punched the 'Open Doors' button, wondering why those who designed the building could not label the levels correctly. But where was he? And where were these levels?

The door opened.

Water spilled into the elevator up to his knees. Stepping out, Carl found himself in a partially flooded corridor whose current flowed out of shadow and hurried into darkness. The lights flickered and sparked to reveal scattered floating debris. From somewhere came the sound of trickling as more water added its volume to the stream.

He dropped the bag and again put his hands to his head.

Re-entering the carriage, he hammered the buttons until they shattered in a spray of plastic and metal springs and he kicked them with a water-soaked shoe. Reluctantly, he returned to the corridor and picked up his bag.

For what seemed an endless stretch of time he walked. His legs slogging in monotonous repetition through the stream of dark liquid, each step throwing up another small wake to die before it could disturb the debris. And always in the background was the endless trickling, the waterfall from some distant sink, the pop as an overhead cast its brief glow on the cramped walls before reverting to blackness.

At length from somewhere came a different sound, a humming that seemed to grow. It took on a harshness as from the chaffing of rough skin, and in the background, over and beyond the chaffing, came the whining of motors.

For a minute Carl stood and listened, unable to take his mind off the low-pitched whine that seemed to drift in and out with the breeze. Except there was no breeze. And in time it focused, sounding from behind, from down the corridor.

It was coming.

He walked more quickly. With the sound increasing, Carl soon cast caution aside and strove frantically to escape the corridor before whatever it was that made those sounds could arrive. At length an open gateseal hove into view and he came to the portal and raced through.

He halted.

Across a wide shallow lake stood a crowd of people

on an upraised platform admiring two Land Rovers to the music of an orchestra. Laughing without concern, they danced and ate and smiled, at times casting supercilious glances at several water-soaked newcomers who stood hesitantly in their midst.

Carl staggered. "I don't believe it. It's her. Damn, it's her!" He began running, sloshing amid rising water. "Carm! Carm, it's me! Carl! I'm here!" He staggered as if punched by a prizefighter. Still within the lake, he was blocked by an invisible wall.

"This can't be. This can't be real. Look this way Carm you must see me standing here; I'm only a few feet away." He slammed his fists repeatedly upon the invisible barrier. No one answered; none even noticed. He started in pain. Something had cut his leg.

He glanced down to glimpse several fish floating about his feet. Their eyes stared into his with a coldness peculiar to finned predators evaluating prey.

Carl backed away.

More fish collected. They worked their jutting jaws in anticipation.

"No...No!" Swiveling, Carl splashed back into the darkness and plunged into another corridor while behind swarmed a thousand silver jewels, grinning with evil.

A closed gateseal appeared. Desperately, Carl grasped the crank, spun it round, reached for the pull-chain and yanked. The door popped open and the water, which had entirely filled the chamber, crashed out with a torrent, knocking him over and scattering the piranhas. A moment passed and Carl regained his feet, the water now up to his waist. He stared–and moaned.

Out of the chamber burst Ray, Leroy, and Griff on hogs, engines whining as he had earlier heard. A horribly burned Dicker, and Jimbo, with a hole in his chest the size of a fist, seized and held him, while the others stretched out his hand with the tattooed box. Ray lifted a hatchet. His water-soaked face leered with savage glee. With a sickening chop, the hatchet lopped it off. Mounting the organ like a trophy between the handlebars of Griff's Harley, they spun round and roared back into its depths.

Carl staggered, his arm spilling blood like a faucet. About him the susurrus grew deafening as a mass of piranha scrambled, positioning themselves for the kill. He lurched, steadied.

Then they came.

Chapter 12

"Almost time." Carm glanced up from the water to look at the others. Cliff and Ed looked down. When they had poled the raft to the mall's wide dais, several inches had remained above the level of the water. Now the dais and the water were even.

Carm shook her head, "The water won't stop. The entire tunnel is flooding."

Cliff breathed rapidly. "We've got to do something."

"But what?" asked Carm. "I tried to warn them, but they wouldn't listen." She wiped a tear. "They wouldn't!"

"Then we'll have to go it alone," said Cliff. "Find a way out. Just for us. If they want to be stubborn, let 'em die. That's their lookout."

"They won't escape," said Ed. He turned his sad round eyes on them both. "Don't you see? This is what fate had in store for them." He looked around at the celebration. "They've been given a last bit of happiness before their doom arrives. Just like us. We began with a party, and we end with one. We won't get out alive either." He looked at Marlena who stood motionless like a shaman, tears in her eyes. He took her hand in his.

A ripple of water spread across their feet and began to cover the platform. In terror they searched for tell-tale darting objects, and saw none. Yet.

"I'm likin' this even less than before, if that's possible," said Cliff.

Bill lay on a gurney, conscious, but in less pain, the medics having administered a sedative before rejoining the celebration. Unable to remove him from the tunnel till the flooding should recede and the gates unlock, they had placed the gurney next to one of the Land Rovers for transport when the flooding should subside. Despite his bandages, some blood still managed to escape and left a pool on the dais.

Carm found herself eyeing the vehicles. "You know, I don't know if this will help, but if we were to get inside one of those, and roll up the windows, just maybe it would keep the water out. We might gain a few more minutes."

She turned to Cliff. "What do you think?"

"Hey, I'd like to live for those few minutes. Let's do it."

In the distance, metal suddenly ripped with the force of an explosion, followed by several more pops, making Carmen think of the church bells of Notre Dame and how odd it was to hear such a sound in the tunnel. The band's music petered out.

Cliff looked more nervous. "Wh...What was that?"

"I imagine that was the gateseals rupturing."

"Like the Titanic."

She nodded. "Time to mosey?"

"Time to mosey."

Walking swiftly to the nearest of the vehicles, Cliff

and Carm paused beside it, followed by Ed and Marlena. The key was in the ignition, and Cliff wiped his brow in relief.

The Mayor glanced once in their direction, and seemed about to intervene, but paused, interrupted by worried party-goers. Carm watched his face for the change she knew was coming. One moment the Mayor was laughing, at one with life; the next he was surprised, uncertain but still confident; then came shock as the initial torrent of water struck the crowd accompanied by the first screams; then sadness as a score of injured people tried to escape the white demons and failed. Finally–worst of all– raw fear as the Mayor realized that he himself would not be spared.

"Now," yelled Carm. Feeling like a conspirator, she opened the back of the Land Rover and they slid the gurney with Bill into the back, then leaped inside, immediately closing and locking the doors. Carm felt again the pangs of guilt. Was it at times like this that soldiers incur survivor syndrome? When they rush to save themselves, knowing that by doing so they condemn comrades to death? An unsuspected hardness emerged as Carm shelved her guilt for later analysis–only survival mattered now. She *must* survive. For her children, if not for herself.

The first wave of water threw scores of pedestrians off their feet. Most, however, steadied each other and helped the others to stand. The next wave did not strike so much as inundate, and bore in its midst the myriad atoms of death that slashed like a tide of razors. Initially clear, the water now turned crimson from a hundred traumas.

Carm turned the key.

Nothing.

"Damn," yelled Cliff, slapping the console. "That's only supposed to happen in the movies!"

Bill rose on one elbow. With his good leg he kicked the back gate. The motor started. "Go figure," he groaned, and collapsed.

A wave struck the truck and buoyed it. For a moment the vehicle turned a circle supported by the water. "It's turned us toward the pavilion," said Cliff. "Can you turn us back the other way?"

Carm revved the engine. The truck dipped and reconnected the floor of the platform. She twisted the steering wheel and slowly they circled back again.

Some two hundred feet away a ruptured gateseal hung loose, the upper register visible above the water. Carm cupped a hand to shout. "If the water from the rest of the tunnel system is pouring into the mall, maybe air from the mall is pouring back into the tunnels! Do you think this truck can drive us out of here? Maybe we can find some stairs!"

"Could be," shouted Cliff over the noise of the engine. "Look!" He indicated a vertical stove-pipe that thrust clear of the water, soaring above their heads like an antenna. "That's the exhaust. As long as water doesn't get in there, the motor can keep running. That's why they call this all-terrain. It's built to swim."

As in a dream, Carm watched the veneer of civilization fall away from the crowd. The people, who but a moment before had been serene in their knowledge of the secure nature of their refuge, in the next disintegrated into a mob, scrambling for any means of escape. Men abandoned wives; professionals threw away jackets and wallets the better to swim; the able trampled the weak and elderly in their desire to snatch a few more moments of miserable life for themselves.

Two well-dressed men struck the hood. One went under and disappeared. The other screamed, "Thieves! Murderers! Let me in, goddam you!" Mr. Beckman's nails scraped the side of the Land Rover as they slid past.

They came to a row of metal tables, tipping several over and spilling their occupants into the water.

Two bloody fists slammed the windshield. "Let me in!" screamed a distorted face, piranhas hanging from its flesh. "My campaign money! My truck!" The fish drilled into him and the Mayor's body exploded onto the hood and windshield. His corpse rolled off.

Cliff wiped more sweat. "I didn't need that either. Let's make for that doorway."

"No," said a voice from the back seat. Marlena leaned forward. "Do not go there. You are in a safe place. When this is no longer safe, you will find another safe place that floats better than this. When you find it, go there." She sat back, then turned to stare expectantly at Ed.

"Wait!" Ed shouted to Carm. "We can't leave yet!"

"Huh? You gotta take a leak or something?" yelled Cliff. "Man, use a cup."

Ed patted his shirt, then his pants. "My talisman–the Egyptian cross. I dropped it somewhere back there."

"That's history, Ed. Forget it."

"You don't understand." He sounded morose. "I'm history without it. You can forget *me*." He swung open his door.

"Man, don't do that! Them things will get in here."

Ed leaped into the water, stood waist-deep and moved away, searching for his cross.

Marlena's door also opened. She looked at the others. "Dear Ed. How could I tell him of what I had seen of my last moments, since they would also be his? But that's all right. That's why we touched your children at the daycare. Our bodies will die, but now our souls will live, saved by their innocence." Carm stared at them without comprehension. Marlena smiled and hurried after Ed. She and Ed joined hands and together they sank and vanished.

The water now rose quickly. Its surface churned and bubbled with a score of red springs. Clothing crawled eerily past as if possessed, driven by the frantic activity of piranhas beneath. The vehicle lost all contact with the floor and Carm found that she could not steer it, but only drift helplessly.

"Look out!" shouted Cliff.

The other Land Rover floated past, barely missing

them. Overfilled with expensively dressed and jeweled elites attending on personal invitation from the Mayor, it lay too low and was taking on water. The driver gunned the engine in a desperate attempt to compensate. A mall pillar loomed suddenly before them, and the Rover thudded to a stop. The windows disintegrated. Carm could not tell which was the more responsible for the gory result, the shattered wet glass that cut the passengers or the piranhas that promptly attacked. The vehicle sank out of sight.

"I think maybe we should have taken that tunnel!" shouted Carm.

Despite the tight seal of the truck's windows and doors, a steady stream of water flowed into the compartment. "Is it too late?" asked Cliff.

She nodded. Then pointed overhead. Framing the hexagonal glass-work that formed the mall's ceiling, beside the sheets of wind and rain that pelted it, were a dense battery of electric lamps mounted on a series of parallel runners. Peering into the corners behind the lamps, Carm thought she could detect a level intervening between the outside ground and the lamps. As the water continued to rise, she saw that she was correct. Running out of this level, power lines crisscrossed the ceiling of the mall, for the most part embedded in the structure that supported and framed the plastiglass panes.

"Are you thinking what I'm thinking?" shouted Carm.

Cliff glanced up. "I hope not."

"If this water doesn't crush us against that hard glass,

then we might first be electrocuted. If we don't sink first. Unless we first get eaten."

"How are you on a good day?"

She smiled. "Bill, are you still with us?" She accelerated in an attempt to avoid more floating tables that threatened to pulverize the windshield.

"Yeah, I'm still here."

"How can we avoid those power lines?"

Bill stared at the water lapping just inches from his face. The floor of the mall was now far below, entirely inundated, and the ceiling was rapidly approaching. Several piranhas sniffed around the back of the vehicle, attracted by the smell of blood inside. "Go straight through the glass. But no chance of doing that."

"Are the power lines hot? Won't the water short them out when it hits? And what happens to us if it does?"

"Yeah. They'll short out. And there's enough power there to light up half the city. But the fail-safe will kick in first. So the main power lines will fizz and then give out a moment after the water reaches them."

A look of excitement settled on Carm. "Wait a minute. Why didn't I think of this before?" She looked at Cliff and Bill. "What if the power lines don't switch off automatically? What will happen to the piranhas?"

"What are you getting at?" asked Cliff.

Bill rubbed his temple, struggling to speak while controlling the pain, but spurred on by the growing concentration of jaws snapping at the windows. "There'll be another fail-safe further up the grid, but I would say those power lines would stay hot for at least a minute, and maybe several. But if you're thinking what I think you're thinking, forget it. Not only fish, but every living thing that's in this water when that happens is gonna be as well done as a Texas tan. Including everyone in this truck."

"And if the fail-safe kicks in? No electrocution, but we die anyway when the water catches us against that glass and steel up there. And later when they drain the tunnel, the piranhas will swim out with the water into the drainage system. They'll infest the whole coast."

"They'll die soon, Carm. Wrong climate."

"Can you be sure? No one has ever introduced thousands of piranhas of a single species into the coastal marshes before. Even if they die after a couple of years, they'll kill dozens more people first. Or maybe they'll become endemic and just keep on killing. Can we take that chance?"

"So what are you saying?"

"No, she's right," said Bill. "We're dead anyway. We need to find some way of disabling that fail-safe switch so the electricity will kill everyone in the mall. And we need to make certain that all the piranhas are here inside so the power lines will kill them."

"Wait a minute. I'm with Terry now. I never signed up to take a bath with no live power lines."

"You have no choice, dude. We're stuck in here together." Bill smiled at Carm. "Well, Miss Ma'am, this steer has been one helluva ride. It's been a party to tell the grandkids about. And I know exactly how to get every goddamn razor-jawed fish in this entire goddamn gulch to come a-runnin'. And that's to ring the dinner bell louder'n it's ever been rung before." With that, Bill proceeded to unwrap the bandage from his leg. Soon the still-bleeding stump was exposed, and Bill took a handful of blood and smeared it on the inside of one window. "And yep, sometimes I do cuss."

Carm smiled.

Bill smiled back. "Now if that don't put the hollerin in the hollerin woman, I don't know what will. Look at them suckers move! There's thousands now!"

Carm looked forward again. Tears came to her eyes, and she bit her lip. Now that she had exhausted herself in a night of frantic attempts to survive, now that she had lost all hope and it had become apparent that her best efforts must fail, a peculiar calm settled and she found that she no longer was so afraid. She knew what she must do, and admired Bill for his bravery, and only hoped that Cliff could find it in him to accept his fate as calmly. Cliff eyed the growing swarm of piranhas that tapped the windows all around, gnashing for his flesh.

Calmer than she had felt in weeks, Carm found that her thoughts were not of the piranhas, nor with her companions, nor even with how or why she had come to such a pass, but with two sprightly children, whose faces floated before her eyes, two joyful souls whose lives forever intertwined with hers, and whose faces she knew would be in her eyes till her dying breath, and whom she believed–had to believe–still lived.

She could see them even now, the lovely elfin Cheyenne, whose cheerful innocence and talents had filled her days with joy. And the impulsive Burke, who inspired her to surmount ever greater obstacles and challenges in proving her love for him. Then the water on the windshield cleared and she wondered how their faces could be so precisely drawn as if her mind had constructed photos of them and projected those photos onto the water before her.

Carm trembled. For a moment she feared that her confusion had returned, and that the Thing in the depths was tormenting her again with unreal images, but this was no ghostly image; they *were* here. Directly in front of the truck out of the shadows and into the headlights floated an outlandish raft of wood, wire and volleyballs lit up by a handful of road warning lights. Leaning on the truck's horn, she was surprised to hear it belt out a joyful sound and she waved frantically until both angelic faces beamed in recognition.

She turned to the others. "Marlena knew. *They* knew. She said we were to take our opportunity when it came. And here it is." Reaching up, she unlatched the roof cover, and swung it open.

"Here, darlings! Paddle as hard as you can!" She pulled the truck alongside the raft.

Bill tied up his leg again. With a hand from Cliff, Carm helped Bill climb through the roof and onto the raft. Carm then stepped carefully on board. She held out her hand.

"Not me," Cliff shook his head. "You may make it, but those rafters look a lot more friendly to me than either that raft or our little friends below." As they watched, Cliff leaped from the Land Rover's roof to the lowest level of rafter intersecting one of the pillars and climbed. He vanished in the shadows among the struts as the truck puttered into darkness.

For a minute Carm and Cheyenne and Burke hugged each other in silence. Bill lay and stared.

"Did you think you would never see me again?" Carm asked.

They shook their heads. "No. We knew you would come. Did you?"

"I was afraid I would not. I should have had more faith."

Again they hugged.

Bill nudged Carm. She looked at him.

"Carm, them fish are all here. In the mall."

She stared at him without comprehension, wiping away tears.

"And the water is about to hit the power lines."

She nodded. "And nothing will happen…"

"Because the fail-safe switch will kick in like a mule and shut down the power lines."

"Yes."

"There is a way to stop that fail-safe from kicking in. See that? That gray button just above the switch disables it."

"What are you proposing?"

"If someone can somehow punch that button, then the fail-safe won't work, the power lines won't shut down, and those fish will be cooked like a Cajun boudin, but we'll be protected on this raft by the volleyballs and plywood. Get me close to that pillar, and I'll climb up like Cliff did, and punch that button."

"Bill, that's impossible. You couldn't even climb out of the truck by yourself. You've lost a lot of blood."

"But it's like you said, if these fish get out, they'll kill a lot more people. And you can't do it. You've got your kids to think of. The fact is, someone has to climb up there and push that button. And darn quick."

"Someone?" said Burke. "Would a little artificial intelligence qualify as someone?" Picking up Mr. Robocopter, Burke flipped on the drone and powered it up.

"Do you think you can hit that button from here?" asked Carm.

"'Here' is not as far away as it was a minute ago," said Bill. "We're rising fast. In another moment, the power will shut down and we'll be in darkness again."

"Silly Mother," said Burke. "Our car window is no larger than that button." He squinted. "Well, maybe a little larger." He took a deep breath and picked up the transmitter. The rotors accelerating, the drone rose vertically up and then spun around the quickly shrinking interior of the uppermost reaches of the mall. Deftly, Burke guided it around several pillars and rafters, coming to a hover just before the dull gray button.

Without warning, the lights died. Like a blanket, darkness covered them so that Carm could see nothing except the dull light of the road sticks. She caught her breath.

"That's not them!" yelled Bill. "It's just the initial power lines. Go for it, kid!"

From somewhere the drone buzzed, a mechanical insect in the dark. A thump sounded and the buzzing was extinguished in a single splash. They looked at each other.

Five seconds passed.

Ten seconds.

Innumerable piranhas now ringed the small raft, their teeth puncturing volleyballs, their scales fraying the ropes.

With a spray of water, a hugely muscled man sprang suddenly from the depths. Piranhas clinging to his horribly mangled body, and with Carl's wedding picture clutched in one hand, Cole grabbed Carm by what remained of her blouse.

"Pretty boy lied!" he bellowed, "Pretty boy lied!"

At that moment the mall lit up with the energy of an exploding fireworks factory. Sparks flooded like a hundred Fourth of July's, singeing their hair, and shattering the plastiglass ceiling, and they watched as the multitude of piranhas stood on end twisting convulsively in its current, their jaws snapping on air. Cole stiffened, his eyes rolling up. For a full minute the macabre dance continued until at last the current shut off as suddenly as it had begun. Bill clubbed Cole with the Tic Tac Toe board, and Carm's foot dislodged his grip on her blouse and the raft.

He returned to the depths.

"Who the hell was that?" blurted Bill.

Carm shrugged. "Someone who missed the party?"

The mall plunged again into darkness. But the darkness was no longer complete, for from somewhere a faint glimmer of light had appeared, shining on their faces through the shattered remnants of the ceiling. Dawn was coming.

As the level of the water continued to rise, to flow at last through the gaps in the roof, the city was surprised to see emerge into the light, in the midst of its central plaza, a ragged ill-constructed raft, with a woman and two children perched haphazardly on its surface, clinging tightly to an object. Once it came to rest, outstretched hands helped them and their injured companion to safety, and, with the sun shining gloriously above, Cheyenne and Burke opened their fingers to gaze upon the luckiest of lucky charms–a golden locket framing a smiling picture of Carm.

Chapter 13

The sun was up and the morning passing when the elevator to the Lab rang and Ruben glanced nervously at the doors. They opened. An ambiguous half-smile, half-smirk on his face, Cliff exited, carrying a suitcase. He hesitated until he saw Ruben. His eyes lit in recognition.

"We must hurry," said Cliff. "It won't do for us to be seen together, in this place. Or for the name of my company, Kwest Lab, to be associated with what has happened here."

"Do?" Ruben wiped sweat from his brow. "It would take a grand jury an hour just to list the charges."

"They won't bother when they find out you've disappeared. Do you have your plane ticket?"

Ruben tapped his inside coat pocket. "One hour. Then I'm on my way to South America." He looked suddenly cagey. "No one needs to know exactly where."

Cliff smiled. "Good. That's smart. That's what I like about you, Ruben. You're always smart. And you've done a good job, keeping me informed about Alice and Gary." Cliff chuckled. "If only MacDonald had known what his little love interest was up to–and how that thief Gary was working behind his back, while supposedly working for *him*. The news would have killed MacDonald–if the storm had not already cut him to pieces when it blew in the twelfth floor window. Of course, I made sure that Mac-

Donald received no help for his wounds." His eye wandered about the Lab. He lowered his voice. "They are not...yet?"

Ruben shook his head. "That's why I'm so nervous." He walked to the window opening on the tank warehouse, Cliff following. They peered through. Tied to two chairs with gags in their mouths were Alice and Gary. Both had large discolored lumps on their heads, with blood pooling about them. They looked barely conscious. "I don't like this," Ruben continued. "I know it's too late to undo what we've done, so let's just get it over with, so I can get the hell out of here."

"Why so squeamish?" asked Cliff. "We've done nothing but a little industrial espionage. I didn't *kill* Nicholas MacDonald—I just let him die. And all you've done is restrain two vicious criminals, a sort of citizen's arrest. Just think of what they did, releasing those piranhas on all those innocent people! You're doing the public a service by eliminating the likes of them."

"Yeah. Well, after all that's happened, I was almost out of a job anyway. It was only a matter of time before Carm or Alice or MacDonald discovered what I was up to." Ruben looked curiously at Cliff. "What was it like? In the tunnels?"

Cliff looked suddenly morose. "You've no idea..." He glanced towards the back of the tank room. "In there... in the deep dark places..."

He shook himself. "Well, you could not prevent Alice

and Gary from releasing the piranhas, but you did manage to conduct several months of secret research on the Array for Kwest Lab, which has put us years ahead of Primal Lab. Our experimental Marine Hybrid genechip has now been fully tested and is ready for production, while they are still stuck on insects."

Ruben nodded. "It wasn't easy testing it while keeping Alice and Carm from learning what I was up to. The way it kept triggering those quarantines. I even had to replace some good transformers with faulty ones just to throw them off. It was a good plan to test Primal Lab's piranha genechip at the same time in case our true project was exposed."

They returned to the Array's console.

"So where is my Marine Hybrid genechip?"

Ruben handed it to Cliff. "It has never left my person since you gave it to me four months ago."

Cliff inspected it with the joyful eye of a new parent. He kissed it and placed it in his pocket. Rubbing his fingers together, Ruben rocked on his heels expectantly. Laying the suitcase flat on a desk, Cliff opened it to reveal stacks of cash.

"One million dollars." Cliff closed the suitcase and handed it to Ruben.

Ruben patted it, grinned, and placed it on the Array console. "That's a lot of money. It would take a grunt like me decades to make this much, even with my Ph.D."

"If you knew how much money my company saved by

producing a marketable product using our competitor's time and facilities instead of our own, this amount would seem puny." Cliff looked up. "By the way, I'm all turned around. Which way to the parking garage?"

Ruben pointed to the tank room. "Right next to us, as the crow flies. The other gateseal in the tank room leads directly to it. But you have to switch elevators and take the one by MacDonald's office."

"You reprogrammed the computer to eliminate the quarantine?"

Ruben nodded. "We can leave any time now. And now that the tunnel is completely flooded we can open the gate and flood the entire Lab according to our plan. The Marine Hybrid algorithm has already been encrypted and transferred online to Kwest Lab's computers."

Cliff beamed approval at Ruben. "Excellent. You've done very well. Set the timers to release the gateseals in five minutes." Ruben stepped to the Array console and clicked the keys. In a few moments he was done.

"Now let's go," said Cliff.

They turned.

"Oh." Cliff paused, snapped his fingers. "Almost forgot." He turned back to Ruben. "Could you check their clothing for anything that might identify us. We can't have any incriminating evidence lying about after they're dead!"

Nodding again, Ruben opened the gate to the tank room and entered. He called out from within, "No, there's nothing. I removed whatever I thought might identify us earlier–"

The submarine door between the Lab and the tank room slammed shut. The crank turned. Locked inside the warehouse, Ruben walked slowly to the window. He stared through the glass, confusion on his face.

Cliff smiled at him. "Oh, Ruben, Ruben. I'm sorry to have to do this, buddy. But, you see, I can't have any incriminating *witnesses* around either!" He chuckled. "No hard feelings," he grinned.

He walked to the console and picked up the suitcase. As the timer on the gateseal to the tunnel system beeped, and water from the tunnels suddenly poured into the tank room, Cliff slid Kwest's new genechip into the Array. Behind him, Ruben saw, and silently screamed.

"Yes, old friend, this *is* the Marine Hybrid genechip. What's the point of pure research without actually testing the product? I have to know that a creature whose DNA was assembled from every major predatory marine animal will actually produce a living, breathing subject." He chuckled again. "*Breathing*...well, you know what I mean. The point is the Array now has all the information it needs to produce a thousand of these creatures in moments." He looked at Ruben. "In *there*. With *you*!" Cliff laughed again. "These hybrids will make piranhas seem weak and feeble, and when the military hears about this incident, you can be sure the whole thing will be written off as a mere industrial accident, and my company, Kwest Lab, will become bigger than Lockheed."

Cliff looked suddenly serious. "Besides, do you think that I am stupid? You see, Ruben, I know it was not Alice and Gary who released the piranhas on us, but *you*. Yes, my friend, you! When MacDonald died, I found in his pocket a check made out to you for *two* million dollars, with a note thanking you for alerting him to Alice and Gary, and a note from you informing him that you had been contacted by me." He tsk-tsked. "Such a little stool pigeon."

A peculiar chirping and clicking resonated within the tank room, and Ruben twirled round, horror-struck, liquid green shadows playing behind him.

Cliff withdrew the Marine Hybrid genechip and replaced it in his pocket. He picked up the box containing all the Primal Lab genechips and put it under his arm.

"And now I must leave, old friend, as I see you have new guests. In another moment, this gate will time out as well, flooding the entire Array, and I... I must be on my way." He walked to the elevator. "To profits. To fame. To world tours, etcetera, etcetera."

Cliff entered. As the elevator doors closed, the gate-seal to the Lab opened and water inundated the Lab, flooding the Array.

Rising to the top floor of the Institute, Cliff exited the elevator and strode to the offices of Nicholas MacDonald. Hurriedly he rifled through Boss-man's desk, stuffing the suitcase further with corporate and personal papers and whatever else of value he could find. Cautiously, he peered down the hallway. The wind still blew through the shattered windows and the streets below were still flooded, so it was unlikely anyone had yet returned to the Institute. Assured, Cliff closed the suitcase, kissed it, and strode to the second elevator.

Somewhere far below, underwater, two bloody hands reached past floating corpses and green tanks and turned a crank on an old gateseal, then reached up and grasped a rusted pull-chain.

Cliff pressed the button for the parking garage and the elevator swiftly dropped. It hurtled without pause, the levels one by one giving forth their dull metallic click. At length it halted at the level labeled Parking. Cliff stood and waited. The doors remained shut. Impatiently he again pressed the button. Nothing. The fluorescents flickered and sweat beaded on his brow as the nightmares rushed back, memories of the dark tunnels with their evil darting demons resurfacing. With a jerk, the doors opened–he caught his breath. For one infinitesimal moment the water seemed to poise, suspended like a wall from floor to ceiling, the bloodshot eyes of Ruben, Alice, and Gary staring from hideously mangled bodies, framed by a phalanx of silvery scaled creatures with writhing tentacles and gnashing jaws.

Then the depths erupted, and the lights died.

NOTE FROM THE AUTHOR:

Frenzy was written in a marathon twenty days in the wake of Tropical Storm Allison, the greatest flood ever to hit Houston. The storm knocked out power and flooded pedestrian tunnels and the basements of hospitals and universities, trapping many for a number of days, drowning several, and bursting an enormous gateseal that no one had supposed could be breached. The Nicholas MacDonald Cancer Institute has some similarity to Houston's most famous cancer research institute just as the story's pedestrian tunnels mirror Houston's own, with the exception that Houston's tunnels do not stretch under Hermann Park and connect with the Medical Center—yet. The ideas of physicist Stephen Wolfram on cellular automata are real. Check out his book *A New Kind of Science* for details. The original title of *Frenzy* was 'piranhOIa', combining 'piranha' with 'paranoia'. Cute, but 'Frenzy' is better.

—Glenn Lazar Roberts

www.ingramcontent.com/pod-product-compliance
Lightning Source LLC
Chambersburg PA
CBHW050450110726
47899CB00003B/882